'Well, come in... allow her past

The momentum of the moment carried Cate through the door and dumped her in the middle of the room. She turned to face him and realised it was a very crowded room and most of it seemed to be filled with Noah Masters.

Exasperated and half-naked, Noah glowered at her, and Cate moistened her suddenly dry lips. 'The night emergency team have been involved in an accident and we need to find replacement staff for this shift...' Cate's voice trailed off as Noah shrugged his way into his shirt. There was something disturbingly intimate in the way he was steadily arranging his clothes in front of her.

'And you want me to do what?' His words were very soft.

'Find me a doctor.'

Fiona McArthur is Australian and lives with her husband and five sons on the Mid-North coast of New South Wales. Her interests are writing, reading, playing tennis, e-mail and discovering the fun of computers—of course that's when she's not watching the boys play competition cricket, football or tennis. She loves her work as part-time midwife in a country hospital, facilitates antenatal classes and enjoys the company of young mothers in a teenage pregnancy group. You can read more about Fiona on her website www.fionamcarthur.com.

Recent titles by the same author:

FATHER IN SECRET
MIDWIFE UNDER FIRE!
DELIVERING LOVE

EMERGENCY IN MATERNITY

BY
FIONA McARTHUR

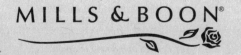

MILLS & BOON®

To volunteers everywhere

First published in Great Britain 2002
Harlequin Mills & Boon Limited,
Eton House, 18-24 Paradise Road, Richmond, Surrey TW9 1SR

© Fiona McArthur 2002

ISBN 0 263 83104 3

Set in Times Roman 10½ on 12½ pt.
03-1102-41929

Printed and bound in Spain
by Litografia Rosés, S.A., Barcelona

CHAPTER ONE

Tuesday 6 March

NOAH MASTERS pushed open the door to Riverbank Hospital and the unmistakable buzz of the internal cardiac arrest alarm sent a bolus of unwanted adrenaline through his body.

He'd sworn he would never work as a doctor in Emergency again, and he hated that staccato buzz. Finally it stopped, and Noah felt the tension ease in his neck as he approached the main office. He could see that the receptionists had returned to whatever had occupied them before the sudden rush of urgent phone calls and he didn't have to wait for their attention.

'My name is Noah Masters, regional CEO. I'm looking for Mr Beamish.' He smiled at the receptionist and the woman blushed and stared up at him. Noah was used to people looking twice at his height but sometimes it irritated him.

She cleared her throat and apologised. 'You're the new chief executive officer? I'm sorry, Mr Masters. Mr Beamish isn't in on Tuesdays, and Miss Glover, the nurse manager, is in a meeting. Perhaps the shift co-ordinator could help you?'

Served him right for not ringing before he came.

Noah mentally shrugged and smiled at the woman again. 'If he or she isn't too busy, that would be fine.'

'I'll page her. She shouldn't be long.' The woman seemed to be all fingers and thumbs, so Noah turned away to survey his surroundings. A Gordon Rossiter riverscape painting took pride of place on the wall and unwillingly his eyes widened in appreciation. The foyer was furnished with a cedar china cabinet and matching chairs. He couldn't resist a stroke of the polished wood and it passed like silk beneath his fingers—hand-turned, he guessed. You had to admit it all made the entrance foyer more warm and homey than he was used to.

Probably all donated, he thought cynically, like most of the equipment in these small country hospitals, but his irritation had eased. Community hospitals had their place, but that didn't change the fact that the big money needed to be spent where the greater population was. He glanced at his watch and the receptionist obviously picked up his impatience.

'Sister hasn't answered her page, but if you'd like to continue around to the emergency department, Mr Masters, I'm sure you'll catch her. If she rings back, I'll tell her you're coming.'

Noah couldn't exactly tell the woman he hated Emergency, so he just nodded and followed the direction of her pointed arm. Just his luck.

When he pushed open the sheet-plastic doors the smells and sounds of a typical morning in Casualty

crowded his senses. Before he could orientate himself, a militant Valkyrie with spiky blonde hair
stopped in front of Noah and barred his way.

'Can I help you?' she said, but it was more of an
accusation than an offer of assistance.

Suddenly the sights and sounds of Emergency receded and Noah eyed her quizzically. She must have
been outside recently, because rain beaded in her
hair and the corridor seemed to vibrate around her
like the electricity that flashed across the heavens
outside the window.

'This is a restricted area.' She used her well-
modulated voice with authority and Noah cynically
admired her technique. Perhaps because he did it all
the time himself.

She squared her shoulders at him. He outweighed
her in muscle by a good twenty kilos, so he wasn't
quite sure what she thought she could do if he decided to proceed past. There was something about
her that made his day brighten and a smile hovered
on the edge of his lips. There could be no mistake
she was a hostile native! A magnificent hostile native but definitely hostile.

'Good morning,' he said. 'I'm looking for the
shift co-ordinator.' Noah smiled his charming smile
but the warrior maiden wasn't like the receptionist
and didn't budge. He resisted the almost irresistible
temptation to move another step forward to see what
she'd do.

She raised her chin, almost as if she'd read his

mind, and Noah had to bite back a smile. He returned her appraisal and gained the impression that the mind behind her really quite beautiful blue eyes was as sharp as the creases ironed into her short-sleeved shirt.

Thick lashes came down and hid her thoughts. 'I'm the shift co-ordinator but I'll be busy for the next half-hour. Are you connected with the hospital?'

His mouth curved a little more. She was interrogating him. He nodded and held out his hand. 'Noah Masters, regional CEO, and you are…?'

Cate had known it! The enemy! 'Cate Forrest, the morning shift co-ordinator.' The suit he was wearing had warned her. But that was the only part of his appearance that tied in with her mental image. She'd known he was coming, she'd just expected a weasel with accountant's glasses.

Unfortunately, he was nothing like she'd imagined. He had a smooth, masculine presence that radiated command and Cate had to tilt her head slightly to look up at him. She didn't like the necessity. There weren't that many men taller than Cate and she wasn't used to it. His hand was out in front of her, waiting, and reluctantly Cate took it.

When his fingers closed around hers in a firm clasp, she returned the shake, frowned and then pulled free as soon as possible.

Her fingers still thrummed. She certainly couldn't say his handshake was as furtive as his visit. The man vibrated with energy! She couldn't stand a man with a limp handshake but that buzz between them was ridiculous. Surreptitiously she wiped her hand on the side of her skirt to remove the tingle.

They stood there and eyed each other like opposing generals, and the silence lengthened. Cate had a suspicion it was amusement she could see in his eyes and it stirred her temper, as a breeze lifted a tiny pile of leaves. Yes, he rattled her, she admitted grudgingly. She was usually the one in control. One minute in his company and she could tell he wouldn't be as co-operative as Mr Beamish was to her plans.

She steered Noah Masters around and back out through the plastic doors to the corridor. 'I'm sorry, I don't have the time for a formal tour today. Perhaps you can arrange something later with Mr Beamish?'

Noah's smile was winning but it bounced off Cate. 'This isn't a formal visit, Sister Forrest. I'm not inspecting Riverbank, I'm just gaining a feel for the place.'

Cate raised her eyebrows delicately. 'How interesting.' You can get a feel just by poking around, can you buster? She only just kept the words from her lips. The pager clipped on her belt emitted an insistent beep and she glanced down to see the phone extension displayed on the mini-screen. It was the accident and emergency main desk. 'Excuse me.

I must answer this call. The cafeteria is on this floor if you would like some lunch.'

Noah inclined his head. 'Perhaps I'll see you on my travels later?'

You'd better believe it. 'We're a small hospital. I imagine you might,' Cate said dryly, and walked away to answer the page.

Noah watched her stride away, her straight back not apologising for her exceptional height and the gentle sway of her hips more provocative, he guessed with a grin, than she intended. She wasn't a dainty, helpless female like Donna had been—totally the opposite, in fact—but she was arresting.

His lips twitched. She actually looked like she wanted to arrest him!

Noah turned back towards the cafeteria with the smile still tugging on his lips. This visit to Riverbank could be more interesting than he'd anticipated.

Cate's head was high. Big city sleaze. He was a big man all over, most of it muscle. Broad-shouldered and deep-chested, and she wouldn't like to meet him in a dark alley. Cate realised it could be a problem to keep her antipathy towards him under control. There was something about him that made her bristle, apart from his obvious threat to Riverbank. But it was a worry what the snoopy Noah Masters was really doing, and how much of a disadvantage to Riverbank it could be to leave him unsupervised. She looked at her watch and sped her footsteps. Hopefully he'd linger over his lunch and she'd be able to find someone to keep an eye on him.

As Cate entered the emergency department, the activity was centred on an elderly gentleman and her footsteps quickened in concern. Mr Beamish, the present CEO of the hospital, was lying on a trolley, obviously in a lot of pain. Judging by the splint still attached to his leg, the problem would affect the man she'd just left. Hell. When it rained it poured.

Casualty Sister Moore turned to Cate with her usual calm. 'Well, that saves me answering the phone. Thanks for coming. Mr Beamish has just come in. He has severe hypothermia and a probable fractured femur.'

Cate nodded and smiled gently at the older man's pale face as he almost blended in with the white pillowcase. 'Hello, Mr Beamish. You've come to the right place for some tender loving care. We'll get you fixed up as soon as we can.' She didn't mention Noah Masters—it was the last thing the poor man needed to know!

Stella Moore followed her out to the nurses' station. 'The ambulance officers just brought him in. He slipped over on his cattle-grid this morning and his wife didn't realise he was in trouble for at least a couple of hours. Mr Beamish had to lie in the rain until she found him, and he's pretty shocked.'

Cate's face clouded for a moment before she said, 'It must have been horrific. Hopefully he won't get pneumonia.' She picked up the phone and glanced out of the window. Water streamed off the pane as she waited for her call to be answered. 'My dad says we're in for a flood and I wouldn't be surprised.'

Stella winced. 'Don't say that. We've just recarpeted our house.' Cate nodded sympathetically. She thought of her parents' farm and the cattle that would have to be moved if the river rose too far, then shelved that problem for after her shift. The telephone just kept ringing so she dialled the nurse manager's number again and finally Cate's immediate superior answered.

Cate left the notification of Mr Beamish's accident with her, along with the news of Noah Masters's appearance.

Miss Glover's voice was hurried. 'I'm in a meeting. Show Mr Masters around if you have time, Cate, please.'

Cate screwed her nose up at the phone and reluctantly agreed.

Her pager beeped and she glanced at the number on the screen. She looked at Stella. 'Anything else you need for the moment, apart from Mr Beamish's old medical records?'

'No. But a lunch-break wouldn't go amiss when you get a minute.' Stella rubbed her hollow stomach and Cate grinned back at her.

'No problem. I'll get the old records, dash over to Maternity to answer this call and come back as soon as I finish there.'

By the time Cate had procured some out-of-stock drugs for Maternity and relieved emergency staff for their lunch, she was in dire need of sustenance herself.

When she entered the cafeteria Noah Masters was the only person left in the room. On the point of leaving, he hesitated, then walked towards her to refill his cup.

Some people took extended lunch-breaks. Cate chewed her lip. She wished he'd left, which was strange considering her previous decision that someone needed to keep an eye on him and she was supposed to show him around.

'The coffee must be good if it's kept you here this long.' Cate snapped her mouth shut on the you-don't-have-anything-better-to-do implication, but it was clear to both of them what she meant.

He raised his eyebrows at her comment and his smile, devastating as it was, was all on the surface. 'The company was good. Your *staff* are very friendly.' The inference was clear.

She supposed she deserved that but she didn't trust him or his smile. She mentally shrugged. She'd never been good at dissembling so most people knew pretty quickly how she felt.

Obviously her staff hadn't realised this man was a wolf casing the flock. She bristled. 'The nurses who work here are wonderful and it always amazes me how they keep their spirits and standard of care up, considering such low funding and the workload expected of them.' By number-crunchers like you, she almost said.

He accompanied her back to the table and on the surface he still didn't seem particularly ruffled. 'Hmm, maintaining a budget is always going to be difficult in a small establishment.'

As if here at Riverbank they didn't try! Cate narrowed her eyes as she set her cup and plate carefully on the table. 'But less important than actually continuing the service.' She paused to let her words sink in. 'Personally, I don't give a hoot for your budget. My concern is maintaining the standard of care the people of this valley deserve—without having to leave the area to get it—and the sooner money is put in its proper perspective, the better.'

His face remained expressionless and she marked another point against him. The guy probably didn't have emotions—just numbers running around inside his computer brain. And she knew he'd been a doctor before he'd taken up administration, which didn't make any sense to her.

He waited until Cate was seated and then sat down. At least he had manners, she grudgingly acknowledged.

Noah set his cup down. 'Unfortunately budgets are a fact of life.'

'Or you'd be out of a job,' she muttered. He turned his head to look at her fully and his eyes flared briefly at her comment. She became sidetracked by the realisation that his chocolate brown eyes could freeze to almost coal black when he was annoyed. The air temperature dropped about ten degrees. She blinked. 'I'm sorry. You were saying?'

For a moment he looked to be inclined to follow up her previous comment but then, with only a brief cryogenic glare, decided against it and reverted to business mode. 'I was saying that budgets are a fact of life and while it's your job to maintain patient services, it's my job to streamline the process cost effectively. The money should go where the needs are greatest. Perhaps we could agree to the necessity for the other person's job.'

The deep timbre of his voice sent an unwelcome shiver across Cate's shoulders. He could be persuasive and she could just see him at a boardroom table, smiling winningly at weaker individuals. She wasn't fooled, though.

In fact, she wasn't temperamentally suited to this conversation. She was more of an action person. Let the official party chat with him. There was no way she could carry on a rational conversation with this guy and not get indigestion. Cate pushed aside the second half of her sandwich and took a last sip of her coffee.

There were still the orders to show him around. 'Is there any area in particular you'd like to see while I have a spare moment, Dr Masters?'

A tiny crease appeared above his right eyebrow at the title. 'If you've finished...' He glanced down at the meagre lunch left on her plate and then away. 'I'd like to see the maternity ward.'

Grimly Cate rose and carried her crockery back to the dish trolley. 'Do you have a special interest in Maternity, Dr Masters?'

Noah winced again at her calling him 'Doctor'. He wished she wouldn't do that. He was never going back to practising medicine. Then he considered the question. Despite the fact that it was the least offensive thing she'd said to him, he knew the question was loaded. He couldn't believe this woman. He'd met people who'd disliked him before, not often, but none as aggressively against him as she was. And she did aggression well. He'd had to struggle with his temper twice already and he couldn't remember the last time that had happened. He'd been controlled like a machine since Donna had died.

He chose his words carefully. 'I believe Maternity can be the showcase of the hospital. Front-line public relations are an important facet of any hospital's success.' And the most common area of overspending. But he didn't say it.

Public relations led back to the dollar again, Cate correctly deduced, and shrugged.

When they walked into Maternity two of the room buzzer lights were on and the nursery was lined with bassinets in which most of the tiny occupants were crying. Mothers with their babies in their arms, crowded around the sink as they waited for weighings and baths.

Noah frowned. 'Where are all the staff?'

Cate almost snorted. '*Both* midwives are doing fifty things at once.' She felt like saying, Can you see anywhere to save money here? But she didn't. Well done. What control, Cate. She patted herself on the back then moved away from him to punch some numbers into the phone.

'Hi. It's Cate Forrest here. Can you send Trudy over to Maternity to help in the nursery for an hour, please? Yes, they're snowed under.' She smiled into the phone and he realised he hadn't seen her smile before. It lit her face with a sweetness that warmed the ice around his heart. She had a smile that reached the corners of the room and shone up the walls. Noah wondered what it would feel like to have that wattage directed solely at him. It would be a smile worth waiting for. He blinked and refocused on the ward around him.

'Thanks,' she said to whoever was on the phone. 'I owe you one.'

One of the midwives came out of the birthing unit and grinned at Cate. 'Two new admissions, both in established labour, right on bathtime, and four babies are waiting for discharge weighings.'

'Trudy is coming over for the nursery. Have you guys had lunch?'

Noah nodded at the mothers who walked past as Cate rearranged staff. He listened to her acknowledge the good job the midwives were doing with the workload and then she proceeded to address several of the mothers by their first names and enquire about their other children. She seemed to know and have one of those smiles for everyone. Except him.

But, then, he guessed she was a people person. He wondered if he still had that knack after two years in administration. Had he lost the knack of emergency surgery, too? Noah squashed that last thought down ruthlessly, and the guilt that rose with it.

Cate caught him studying her and excused herself from the mother she was speaking to. She moved across to his side with the light of battle in her eye. 'Do you advocate breastfeeding, Dr Masters?'

Under attack, Noah looked around at the mothers watching him. 'If at all possible, of course I do,' he said cautiously.

'So you'd agree it's important that first-time mums in particular have access to help for at least the first few days after the baby is born to establish lactation? Especially if you believe that breastfeeding is best for babies.'

A glimmer of light appeared and Noah narrowed his eyes. Before he could ask if this had to do with his suggestion to shorten postnatal stays, she continued.

'Were you aware that, unlike larger hospitals, Riverbank clients don't have access to early discharge follow-up by midwives? Only overworked early childhood nurses?'

Her blue eyes bored into his and he had to admire her passion, if not her subtlety.

'No, I wasn't aware of that.' He was going to continue but Cate cut him off.

'Or that we have some of the best long-term breastfeeding rates in New South Wales?' She looked justifiably proud about that.

She was like a steamroller and from one steamroller to another he couldn't help admiring her—but a public hallway was unfair. 'No. I wasn't aware of that either, Sister Forrest,' he replied sardonically. He didn't understand why he wasn't more annoyed with her. Perhaps it was the obvious undeniable passion she had for her work.

'Pity!' She'd scored her point and was ready to change the subject. 'Seen enough?'

Before he could answer, her pager went off and she was thinking of something else. 'I'm off to Accident and Emergency, Dr Masters.'

He knew she wanted to get rid of him but he wasn't going to be shaken off that easily. 'I'll tag along, then.'

He lengthened his stride to keep up with her, which was quite a startling change from usually having to slow his pace for women. He found himself smiling again—Cate Forrest was certainly different.

Thunder rumbled outside and Noah shook his head as he glanced out of the window to see the sheets of rain falling even harder. 'This is some storm.'

Cate paused and followed his gaze out of the window. 'It's more than a storm.'

Noah frowned. 'Meaning?'

'My father says we're in for a flood—and when a farmer predicts a disaster, it's a definite worry.'

Farmers predicting weather. He'd heard of that but he didn't believe in it. 'So how often does it flood around here?'

Cate turned from the window and started walking again. 'Nineteen sixty-three was a big flood but 1949 was the biggest in recent history. That flood washed right through the centre of town, killed six people and left others stranded on the roofs that didn't wash away. The locals still talk about that one.'

Her pager shrilled and she glanced down and muttered, 'Outside call.' Then picked up the pace again.

'The staff with creek crossings can have problems getting in when it's like this. That will be the first of those who can't get in.' She smiled sweetly at him. 'They get flooded-in leave.'

He frowned. 'Can't you make them stay in town before they get flooded so the hospital will be staffed properly?'

Cate raised her own sardonic eyebrow. 'Perhaps if that was a permanent rule, we could have our hospital staffed properly at normal times?'

He flicked a questioning glance across at her until he realised she was baiting him—again.

A small frown marred her forehead and he realised that he had only a fraction of her attention. Another thing he wasn't used to. 'I'll leave you to it, Sister Forrest. I can see you have your hands full.'

For the first time she smiled at him, and he couldn't help but smile back. As he turned down the opposite corridor towards his car, he acknowledged wryly that all he had to do was leave her and she'd smile.

CHAPTER TWO

AFTER work, Cate tried to concentrate on the road home to her parents' farm in the torrential rain, but it required more attention than she wanted to give. She knew she needed to be less fixated on scoring against Noah Masters and more focused on the rising river and her father's cattle.

Compartmentalising had never been a problem with men before. Even during her engagement she'd been able to parcel Brett up in to one part of her life while she carried on with something else. So why did thoughts of Noah Masters not stay where she told them to? She grimaced. Maybe he was too big.

She couldn't help the image of Noah popping so clearly into her memory. And she couldn't help the awareness of her attraction to him—something she'd been fighting all day—from stealing her concentration.

Cate's utility rattled over the cattle-grid and the sheets of rain made it hard to make out the figure sitting in the wheelchair on the verandah. She waved anyway as she drove past and parked in the garage. Shaking rain off as she came, Cate hurried up the verandah steps to drop a kiss on her father's leathery cheek. 'Hi, Dad.' William Forrest was another big man and her heart ached to see him confined to the wheelchair. Oddly, he'd adapted to being paralysed better than his family had.

'Hello, love. River's rising,' he said, and they both turned to look towards the bottom paddock river flat. The thickened brown snake of the river was spreading slowly across the lowest areas. 'Your mother's trip to town yesterday was in good time. We've enough supplies for a month.'

'Hopefully the rain won't last a month.' Cate grinned wryly at her father and laid her hand on his shoulder. 'I'll change after my coffee and move the cattle up to the house paddock.'

His bushy white eyebrows drew together. 'I thought the fence had snapped up in the house paddock?'

'I fixed it yesterday before I went to work but the gate's only just hanging on.'

He put his hand over hers and gripped it as if to say, Hear me out. 'The farm is too much for you and your mother. I've asked your brother to come home.'

Cate tried not to feel that she'd failed him. Her father shouldn't have had to do that. 'Oh, Dad, there's no point worrying Ben! We can manage. I'll fix the gate this evening.'

William was still very much the head of the family and knew how to be firm. 'It's too much. You're a fine daughter and as good as any man on the farm.

But you have your own life. And I'll need him for the flood, if it comes.' There was no doubt her father believed they were in for a big flood.

Cate turned away and tried not to think about the changes that Ben's return would make. Her brother had left home without a backward glance as soon as he'd turned eighteen. He had chosen to work in the Northern Territory on another man's property, leaving her parents to manage with only her. Cate was really proud that she and her mother *had* managed. They still could—but it was her father's choice. This day couldn't get worse.

'That's good, Dad.' The words nearly stuck in her throat. She'd worry about Ben coming home when, and if, he actually did. For the moment there were things to do before the next two days' shifts at the hospital and she was looking forward to some activity for the restlessness that had been eating at her since she'd driven away from the hospital. She left her father watching the rain.

'How were your shifts, darling?' Cate's mother set two coffees on the kitchen table and sat down to listen. Leanore was a tall woman, though not as statuesque as her daughter, and her hair was more silver than blonde.

Cate's thoughts flew to the regional CEO, and strangely she was reluctant to discuss Noah Masters with her mother. She stared down at the cup cradled in her hands. 'Busy.'

Not one to avoid discussing awkward subjects,

Leanore went straight to the family issues. 'Your father and I are looking forward to Ben's return. It will be wonderful to see him. Are you upset your father asked him to come home?'

Cate couldn't help the tinge of censure in her voice. 'If he stays long enough.'

'Now, Cate. It's been a hard couple of years but Ben is a man now and he wants to come home. He'll be better for the time away. He was too young to take over the huge job that you've done and too old to take orders from his big sister.'

She patted Cate's hand.

'Your father rose above his disabilities and is still the man of my dreams. We have our life and you have yours. We know you've carried the lion's share of the workload for a long time now. You deserve a break. Sit back and let Ben and your father do the worrying without you. Live a little.'

Leanore pushed a plate of home-made biscuits towards her daughter. 'So tell me some good news from the hospital.'

Cate tried to brighten up. 'My friends Michelle and Leif had a lovely baby boy early this morning. He was nearly a Caesarean but beat the doctor to the theatre.' A soft smile crossed her face. 'He's gorgeous.'

She blinked and refocused on her mother. 'And poor Mr Beamish broke his hip on his cattle-grid and I'm dreading the new regional CEO will step into his job until they get someone else.' She glared at the tablecloth. 'I hope it's soon,' slipped out.

'Poor Mr Beamish. I went to school with his wife.' Leanore tilted her head. 'A new regional CEO? What's he like?'

Cate stirred her coffee vigorously and the coffee spun dangerously around in her cup. 'Taller than Dad, looks like he works out, but he's a human logarithm and very much the city boy.' She glared at her coffee. 'He's domineering and annoyingly sure of himself.'

Cate's mother took the spoon from her daughter and set it in the saucer with a clink. 'Interesting.' She smiled to herself. 'He seems to have made a big impression on you. But the last part is a harsh indictment. I imagine the man would have responsibilities that call for most of those qualities. Does he have a name?'

'Noah Masters.' Cate shrugged and took a few sips of her drink before she set it down. 'I don't want to talk about that man. Thanks for the coffee, Mum. I have to fix the gate in the top paddock and move the cattle.'

'Do you want me to come?' Leanore started to untie her apron, still with a small smile on her face.

'No. Thanks.' Cate thought she may as well do this last job before Ben came home. 'I need to get out and I'll call if I need help.' She slipped the family mobile phone onto her belt. It was her father's decree that anyone in the paddocks carry it in case they needed help. Three years ago he'd lain all day with a broken back when the branch of a tree had fallen and crushed his vertebrae. With the farm work falling to Cate and Leanore now that Ben had gone, he could keep in contact with them from the house. Cate would have carried anything to get out of the house and burn off some energy.

Wednesday 7 March

When Cate arrived at work that afternoon, she'd packed a case with enough clothes for a week. Her father had predicted she wouldn't get home for a while.

'Noah Masters had better watch out!' Cate dropped the report of the regional hospitals' meeting, which she'd taken home to study, down on the desk. It hit with a clap similar to the thunder outside.

She impaled her drover's oilskin on the old-fashioned hatstand as if she were hanging Noah Masters out to dry on it.

'And happy Wednesday to you, too, Cate.' Diminutive Amber Wright stood up to flick the door shut behind her friend for some privacy. The nursing supervisor of the previous shift at Riverbank Hospital shook her head. 'You're like a whirlwind some days, Cate. You make me dizzy.'

Cate dried her hands on the damp scarf she pulled from around her neck and hung that up, too. 'Maybe the weather makes me mad.'

'Yeah, right.' Amber had her head in her hands.

Cate tucked her handbag away. 'That good, is it?' said Cate as Amber lifted her head. Her friend nodded.

'Ten staff called in flood-bound and we're still five down without replacements, but it could have been worse. Most are flooded in while some are banking on staying home so they don't get flooded out of their own homes.' Amber sighed.

'Plus, I have to be at preschool in twenty minutes and barely have time to fill you in on what's happening on the wards.'

Cate looked up quickly. 'That's a bit early. Cindy's not sick or anything, is she?'

'No. I have a meeting with the teacher.' Amber looked at her watch and Cate interpreted her frown. Amber really couldn't afford to upset the teacher at the preschool Cindy attended most days while her single mother worked.

Cate picked up her pen. 'Heaven forbid that you keep the teacher waiting. Come on. Fire away and we'll get you out of here on time.'

Amber shuffled the papers and pushed her glasses back up her nose. 'I've had orders to encourage the doctors to discharge as many as they can to lighten the load, but most of the people who could go don't have the support at home, and home care is a bit iffy should the highway be cut off.'

Cate leaned forward but her voice was soft. 'So

whose orders were they?' As if she didn't have an inkling.

'Noah Masters.'

'I'm just about sick of his directives. I found out he's a doctor of medicine, and has only been involved in the corporate side for two years. Apparently he's shooting up the administrative totem pole at a great rate of knots.' She screwed up her nose. 'How could a doctor leave medicine and become a number-cruncher?'

'Excuse me?' Amber pulled a face. 'You only work half your time as a midwife and the other half in administration.'

Cate sniffed. 'Totally different. I need the quick shifts. An afternoon shift followed by a morning shift lets me work on the farm. If there weren't enough midwives I'd go back to full-time midwifery like a shot.'

Cate watched as Amber punched the last of the entries for staff changes into the computer. 'The office part of this job is a pain but as for shift co-ordination...' Cate shrugged '...I believe I can make a difference if I ensure that everything runs smoothly.'

'It's true. The place runs like a watch when you're on shift.' Amber shot her an urchin grin. 'But you also like being boss. Hell, I was on your tennis team and we had to win or else. One day you're going to meet a man that won't let you boss him around. Maybe it's Noah Masters.'

Cate's laugh sounded more like a snort. 'Somehow I don't see that as prophetic.' She folded her arms and glared at her friend. 'And as for tennis, what's wrong with being champions three years running?'

Amber laughed out loud. 'I rest my case,' she said. Cate acknowledged the hit with a wry smile.

Amber went on. 'Our regional CEO is officially filling in for Mr Beamish.' She looked at Cate. 'He said to call him Noah, which made me laugh a bit as we've probably got a flood on, but he doesn't seem too bad.'

'The man's a walking calculator!' Cate stood up and paced the room.

Amber looked up with interest. 'Then he's a well-packaged calculator.' She shrugged. 'I'd almost welcome his slippers under my bed if I wasn't off men.' She raised a quizzical eyebrow at Cate. 'Struck a few sparks yesterday, did you?'

That was the last thing Cate wanted Amber to think. 'No.' The word came out louder than she'd intended and Cate fought not to blush. 'It's not a matter of liking or disliking. The guy is a threat to Riverbank—and if he had his way our hospital would be downgraded to cottage hospital status.'

Amber blew a raspberry. 'You don't know that.'

Cate didn't meet Amber's eyes. 'Well, I don't want to find out the hard way. Can we leave Noah Masters, please?' Cate sat down. 'What else is happening here today?'

Cate couldn't mind Amber's teasing. She couldn't remember a time when Amber hadn't been in her life. They'd shared rag dolls and horse blankets since kindergarten. Experience told Cate that something else was bothering her friend.

Amber smiled but Cate still felt she was stalling, which wasn't like her. 'Let's get you home. Is something wrong, Amber?'

All amusement left Amber's face and she sighed. 'I'll start with the bad news.' She put her hand out to cover Cate's. 'Iris Dwyer is our critical patient and her friends are with her in the palliative care room, but her son hasn't arrived yet.'

Iris… Cate fought back the sudden dread and managed a professional nod to Amber. But her mind whirled. Iris, not Iris! There was only one reason a patient would be admitted to the hospital's soothing palliative care suite with its very comfortable bed, and Cate didn't want to think about it.

Iris was the sort of woman every girl would have loved having as a mother-in-law. She was certainly everything Cate wanted to be—independent, with a home and farm and a loving son to care for. Mr Dwyer had died some two decades earlier and, far from withering, Iris just seemed even more determined and in control.

And now that would change. Cate acknowledged the sympathetic look from Amber. Iris and Brett had been a big part of her life before the break up of their engagement.

'Brett's mother has terminal cancer?' Cate shook her head in disbelief. 'Why didn't I know she was sick? Why wouldn't she tell me? Maybe I could have done something…'

Amber understood. 'Don't feel bad she didn't tell you. Iris has always been a self-sufficient woman. She must have preferred it that way. I don't think she told anyone before she came in here.' Amber shot a look at Cate to watch for her reaction to the next news. 'Brett will be here soon.'

Cate sniffed. 'Why isn't he here now? He'd better get here in time…' Cate was still reeling from the more devastating news.

Amber sighed. 'You take too much on yourself, Cate. Nobody knew about Iris's illness. She went to Theatre this morning for an abdominal mass and it was an open-and-shut case. Nothing they could do. She's been running the farm up until her admission and it looks like she's organising the way she dies just as efficiently.'

A cold lump settled in Cate's stomach and the back of her throat scratched as she fought to control the surge of emotion that welled. Brett had better make it. While her ex-fiancé was quite capable of behaving less than responsibly, she'd always enjoyed the company of his forthright and capable mother.

Cate sometimes wondered if her fondness for Iris had been half of her attraction when Brett had come back on the scene.

Amber touched her arm. 'How do you feel about seeing Brett again?'

Cate gave a tiny shrug—that was unimportant by comparison. 'Like a fool for ever agreeing to marry him. But apart from that, I feel sorry that he's going to lose his mother.' Cate blinked away the sting in her eyes.

'There's a hard time ahead for him,' Amber said with a catch in her voice, and Cate remembered that her friend had always had a soft spot for Brett. She could have him.

'Poor Iris.' Cate blinked the sting out of her eyes and met Amber's sympathetic gaze. 'You need to pick Cindy up from preschool. I'll find the rest out when I go up and see her later on the ward.'

Amber nodded and glanced at her clipboard. 'Iris is our most critical. The other patients in Medical are slowly improving, which means they're pretty much the same as they were when you went off yesterday. They have two spare beds.

'Theatres are running to time, and Theatre Sister asked, as you were doing a quick shift, if you could take Theatre call tonight as it's her husband's birthday.'

Cate shrugged at the chance of having her eight-hour break between shifts broken by an unexpected theatre case, as it had the last time she'd done the quick shift. 'No problem. Have you marked it down yet?'

'No. But I didn't look for anyone else. Marshmallow centre—that's you—but at least a lot of people owe you favours!' Amber grinned and wrote down Cate's name for the call.

'Surgical?' Cate took the theatre list Amber handed across and scanned the list of operations that had been that morning.

'No spare beds so any emergency admissions or accidents will cause a reshuffle of beds or early discharge.

'Children's Ward has three in with gastroenteritis so don't play with them if you want to spend time helping in Maternity,' she teased.

'And how is Maternity?' Cate settled in the chair.

Amber flicked her reading glasses back up her nose. 'Just how you like it. They have babies coming out of their ears and two more in early labour.'

Cate nodded. 'I love it when it's like that.'

Amber rolled her eyes. 'Intensive Care has three in, all day-two myocardial infarcts, who are progressing well. And last, but not least, Emergency is surprisingly quiet for the moment, but we all know how that can change in the blink of an eye.' Amber put her reading glasses in her case and handed over the clipboard and the large bunch of keys. 'Have fun with Noah Masters. I'll look forward to the next instalment of Cate versus Goliath.'

Amber stretched up and hugged Cate. 'I'm sorry about Iris.'

Cate returned the pressure. 'She's a wonderful

woman and deserves more—but thanks.' She pushed
Amber towards the door.

Cate shivered in sympathy as she watched her
friend cross the car park from the office window.
The rain was pelting down and Amber's umbrella
turned inside out from the wind as she struggled to
get the keys into her car lock.

Cate envied Amber her beautiful daughter but not
Amber's marriage to the domineering man she'd di-
vorced.

Cate dreamed of a home and family more than
anything, and she'd thought she'd found the answer
with Brett. But her great love affair hadn't worked
out either. Cate didn't waste any sympathy on herself—she should have known better. Brett had ruled
by emotional blackmail and she'd been lucky they
hadn't married. She thought of Brett's mother and
sighed. Poor Iris.

She painfully rolled her shoulder. She'd pulled a
muscle yesterday trying to straighten the top paddock gate. Served her right for being too stubborn
to call her mother for help.

And now it looked like Noah Masters had moved
into Mr Beamish's office indefinitely. Life was suddenly too much.

She didn't feel like being cooped up in the office.
She needed to be busy and if they were short-staffed,
there would be plenty of work to do.

By late afternoon, Cate had secured relief for ex-
tra-busy wards from the less frantic ones, helped

with the birth of a baby in Maternity, arranged casual staff who lived in town to replace those flooded in for the next shift, and updated the computer with the latest staffing statistics. She'd briefly spoken to every patient and a host of their relatives, and everything was under control. This was what she loved—having her finger on the pulse of the hospital.

By five o'clock she'd made several visits to Mrs Dwyer in her darkened room, and she decided to pop in for a moment before tea. When Cate entered the room the old lady lay so still and quiet that for a moment Cate thought Brett had left it too late. Then she noticed the gentle rise and fall of the sheet covering the frail body and she bit her lip. Iris had only been deeply asleep. The old lady stirred and opened her eyes.

Brett's mother looked frail and it was as if the light had been turned out in her usually sparkling blue eyes. Cate could see that time was short and she felt useless as she stared down at the woman she'd grown to love. 'Can I get you anything, Iris?'

Iris smiled. 'No, darling.' The skin on the older woman's hand was callused from hard work and yellow-tinged with jaundice. But her grip was still strong. 'I'm quite comfortable. Even the dawn chorus of coughing and urinals is different to the birds at home but quite amusing.'

Cate couldn't help smiling, which was what Iris

wanted. 'Would you like some music to drown out the ward clatter? I could bring my CD player in.'

Iris shook her head. 'You do too much as it is and I don't need to add to your load. There'll be plenty of time for music in heaven.' Cate winced and Iris frowned. 'Stop it. I've had a good life and at the moment I'm enjoying the sound of humanity. It's like a radio show and guess-the-secret-sound as I try to recognise a noise. Don't worry about me.'

Iris closed her eyes but she was still smiling and Cate wondered if she'd fallen asleep again. Cate could see from whom Brett had inherited his eyebrows and nose. A shame he hadn't inherited his mother's determined chin. Almost as if she'd caught Cate's thoughts, Iris opened her eyes.

'I'm sorry it didn't work out for you and Brett, for his sake.' Her eyes twinkled briefly. 'As much as I love him, I know he probably would have driven you mad. I've come to think he needs someone to lean on him to bring out his best. But I would have known he was OK with you.' The frail hand tightened in Cate's. 'Look after yourself, Cate. You need to find a strong man to depend on. Sharing the load brings its own strength so if the chance comes, don't fight it too much.'

Cate dropped a kiss on the wrinkled cheek. 'How like you to try and tie up my loose ends as well. Think about yourself for a change. I'd better get on with my work. You rest and mind you tell Sister if the pain gets worse.' Iris shut her eyes and she was asleep before Cate turned away.

Cate tried to regain her composure. Sometimes life was very unfair. She couldn't believe Brett hadn't arrived yet. She'd kill him if he didn't get here in time. She pushed herself off the wall she'd leant her head on and hurried out of the room with her emotions a jumble, and pushed her sore shoulder straight into a solid wall of muscle. Two strong hands steadied her until she regained her physical balance and her traitorous body relaxed for a moment against the man. Her emotional equilibrium was harder to recapture.

'Sister Forrest. We meet again.' Noah's hands loosened as she stepped away a pace but he could still feel the aftershock of her surprisingly luscious body against him.

Noah redirected his gaze from the vulnerable line of Cate's neck to her face as she straightened herself to look at him.

'I'm sorry. I wasn't looking.' The slight catch in her voice sounded strange, coming from the tough cookie of yesterday. In fact, she looked like she was in some pain.

'Did I hurt you?' Noah tilted his head and then reached out to touch her shoulder. She winced and his brows drew together.

She brushed his hand away. 'It's an old bruise and I've just given it a reminder. I'm fine. Was there something I can do for you?'

She didn't look as together today, but she certainly wasn't any friendlier. It had been amazing how many little things he'd remembered about her. Like the way her blue eyes narrowed and then seemed to glow like flashing blue sirens when she was annoyed with him. And how the expressions on her face seemed to shift and change like the sea.

Enough. Noah compressed his lips. He'd spent too much time thinking about her last night and he wasn't going to get bogged down today. But she was a challenge. He refocused on her question.

'I've come up to see how the medical resident went with discharging non-critical patients. I assumed there would have been more clients able to go than we've managed to discharge.'

He watched her close her eyes for a minute to marshal her thoughts. When she opened them he was staring quite openly at her and she glared at him. He'd bet she couldn't help herself. She'd be a dreadful poker player, he thought as he watched more emotions flash across her face when she spoke. 'Those that are still here would be at risk if they were discharged. Until the rain stops we can't guarantee that the community nurses will be able to take them on or that relatives will be able to get to them if they're needed.'

There was that fire and passion for the patients again. He had to harden his heart. 'So what you're saying is that if it wasn't raining you'd be happy to send them home?' She would fight him all the way, but that wasn't a problem. He felt more alive than he had for years—perhaps it was the country air he hadn't looked forward to.

She did look determined, though. 'What I'm saying, Dr Masters, is that an early discharge for these *clients* would most probably result in readmissions—which cost more money by the way—so nothing would be gained by putting them at risk.' She folded her arms across her chest.

'What about the risk here if you have an influx of sick patients and minimum staff to care for everybody? I'll have a list of other possibles anyway, please, Sister Forrest.'

He watched her shrug and realised she probably thought he hadn't heard a word she'd said.

Cate tilted her chin. 'Then it's on your head.'

'That's what my head is here for.' His attempt at humour failed to draw a smile and she stared stonily back at him. He shrugged. He had other things to worry about. 'I assume you're aware that I've taken over from Mr Beamish in the interim as this hospital's CEO?'

'The news had made it to my desk, yes.' She glanced at her watch.

Noah could feel his temper rise. So he was holding her up, was he? 'I hope I can rely on your support during this unsettled time, then.'

'Of course,' she said. So why did he feel that her fingers must be crossed behind her back?

Then she said, 'I always have the hospital's best

interests at heart.' This time her voice wasn't so meek. Her pager sounded and she tilted her chin before moving away.

Noah shook his head. Right. He'd have her support as long as she totally agreed with his plans, and he watched her turn the corner towards Intensive Care without looking back. But she didn't know whom she was up against. He narrowed his eyes thoughtfully at the spot where she'd disappeared from view.

Cate couldn't get away fast enough. Bumping into Noah Masters straight after seeing Iris had left her in turmoil. She'd actually felt comforted by his strong grip on her arms and her step back had been a defence against the inexplicable desire to stay and lean on him for a moment.

Of all the people to feel like leaning on! She needed to get a grip on things. Why hadn't Brett come so she could stop worrying about it hanging over her head? She hoped it wasn't going to be awkward to see Brett but it was the first time face to face since they'd broken their engagement.

Luckily she was busy. The rain continued and the calls from marooned staff members also flooded in. Cate glanced out of the corridor window as she made another trip to Maternity and realised that if the rain kept up she'd be one more person blocked by rising waters from going home. Though after her phone call to her parents earlier, she knew her brother was at home now. They said they'd manage fine without her. She wasn't sure how she felt about that.

Cate pulled open the door to Maternity. Michelle and Leif were going home a day early with baby Lachlan and they were waiting to say goodbye. Early on Tuesday morning, Cate's sleep in the nurses' quarters had been interrupted to set up for an emergency Caesarean section when baby Lachlan's descent through his mother's pelvis had apparently stopped.

To everyone's relief, he'd made his precipitous arrival in the normal way in the operating theatres before the surgeon had scrubbed his hands.

'Lachlan looks much better this morning, Michelle. And so do you.' The new parents looked up and smiled, and Cate's day brightened to see the baby feed contentedly at his mother's breast.

Michelle was small-boned and blonde, and she stroked her son's thick crop of black hair. 'Thanks, Cate. It's amazing how much they change in just two days. He was so blue and his head was such a strange shape when he was born.'

Cate grinned as she remembered the marked moulding of Lachlan's head caused by his squeeze through his mother's pelvis. 'I remember. Thank goodness babies' skull bones are designed to do it. If he'd just tucked his chin in he would have made it much easier on both of you.'

Leif laughed. 'And your sleep. He was such a cone head. When I asked if his head would change shape, the doctor said if newborn heads didn't there'd be a lot of funny looking people walking around town. That's when I knew he was going to be all right.' They all laughed at the mental picture of a town full of people with misshapen heads. 'Everyone has taken such good care of us.'

'And so we should.' Cate had gone to school with Michelle's older sister. The beauty of working in a small town hospital was that she knew most of the patients or at least one of their relatives.

The new parents wanted to make sure they could make it home before their road was cut off.

'Now, you're sure you have enough supplies?' Cate stroked Lachlan's tiny hand as he lay in his mother's arms.

Michelle reached up and kissed Cate's cheek. 'Leif's picked up everything on the list this morning and we have enough stuff to last us a couple of weeks. Hopefully the flood won't linger, but luckily our house is on a hill. At worst we'll be on an island, but I want to be home if that happens.'

'Of course you do. Good luck and hopefully the roads won't be shut long. Remember to ring the ward if you're unsure about anything to do with you, breastfeeding or Lachlan.'

Cate left them to pack the car in dashes through the rain, and got on with her own work, but she couldn't help comparing her life to that of Michelle.

Michelle was five years younger than Cate's thirty years. She already had a husband who adored her and a new son and her own tiny farmhouse on the outskirts of town. It sounded idyllic and Cate sighed.

Something was missing in her life and she could almost see herself ending up alone, with nothing but patients and cows to look after, when all she had ever wanted had been a home and family. Even Iris had had a child and Cate was beginning to wonder if she'd ever have a baby of her own.

Perhaps that fear had been a factor in allowing her relationship with Brett to grow. She'd grown up with the local boys as friends. As casual boyfriends they hadn't seemed to mind the fact that she was better at most things than they had been, but Cate had never found any reason to become heavily involved with someone she'd known.

Until Brett had returned from medical school to complete his residency in Emergency at Riverbank. He'd stormed her citadel with flowers and pretty words and hadn't been intimidated by Cate being in charge—quite the opposite. Their pairing had seemed to suit all round.

Early on he hadn't seemed so self-centred and perhaps she'd encouraged him to expect her to look after him. Iris's comment that Brett needed someone to lean on him to bring out his best could be very true. She'd thought that together they could have made a good life, although to be honest she'd seen herself as the stronger of the two. To achieve a love affair like her parents' might have been stretching the fantasy, but her dream of a caring husband and a home and family had seemed within her grasp.

And Cate had always admired Iris. Over the course of her twelve-month engagement with Brett, she'd stifled the doubts that had crept in occasionally because of that. She wasn't proud of almost marrying a man she hadn't loved. She should really thank her brother Ben for making it impossible for her to follow Brett to Sydney like he'd wanted. With the choice between leaving her parents to manage on their own and her loyalties to Brett, who had wanted Cate to himself, Brett had come a poor second.

But now her future alone seemed to stretch ahead of her. It would be better once Brett was here and she could stop worrying that he might expect to take up where he'd left off—or that she might be tempted…

Speaking of temptation, there had been that feeling of Noah Masters's hands not so long ago, resting gentle but strong on her shoulders. Cate shrugged her shoulders and stormed to her office. Of course the phone was ringing and Cate reminded herself that there was no time for temptation when there was work to be done.

She reached across the desk to lift the phone to her ear just as a shadow darkened her doorway. Noah Masters blew into the room like a hail-filled cloud and seemed to shrink her office to half its size.

CHAPTER THREE

THE pertly rounded rear and long, long legs of Cate Forrest as she leant across a desk was a sight to gladden any hot-blooded male's day. Noah just wasn't used to it happening to him. He'd barely noticed any woman's femininity for the last two years and here he was stifling a wolf-whistle like some callow youth. He must be going potty with the rain.

He dragged his eyes away and took a turn around the room to divert his libido from more of those fantasies of tall, leggy women he'd resurrected since yesterday. He glared out of the window and stoked up the embers of annoyance that had sent him to search her out. The wretched rain still teemed down and the idea of a flood was becoming more believable every day. A brief scenario entered his head of Cate and himself marooned together on an island for a couple of days with nothing to do...

Cate concentrated on the phone call and tried to pretend her heart rate hadn't accelerated at Noah's presence. She had to admit he had a presence—but it was just the *unexpectedness* of his entrance that had startled her. She spoke into the phone and her voice was even. 'Sister Forrest. Nursing Supervisor.' She straightened to perch on the edge of the desk and the phone cord pulled tight as she turned her body to watch Noah prowl around the office impatiently.

Annoyed with how much he distracted her, she tried not to tense as she ignored him to listen to Stella Moore. The emergency sister had called to warn she might be late for work.

Cate's attention returned to the phone call. 'Take care. We'll manage until you both get here. I think it's a great idea to come in together. But if it looks too dangerous, don't even attempt it, Stella. Let me know as soon as you both arrive. We'll probably have to catch up on some shifts if the casuals have to cover for too long so I appreciate you coming. Thanks for the warning and make sure your husband looks after that new carpet. Bye.'

Well, that saved her having to find another experienced emergency sister to work the night shift. Stella had arranged to share a lift with the night resident doctor in his heavy-duty four-wheel-drive vehicle.

She put the phone down gently and glanced up at Noah, who was glaring out of the window again at the weather. 'Yes, Dr Masters?' Cate searched in her memory for something recent she might have done to annoy him, but couldn't come up with anything.

His eyes were more like frozen chocolate this time and his usually beautiful lips were a straight line. 'Sister Forrest, would it be too much to assume that you could have kept at least one free room in the staff quarters for me to sleep in during this crisis? I've just been to the nurse manager for a key and Miss Glover tells me all rooms are taken.'

Cate's brow wrinkled. 'I'm sorry. I've given them to the nursing staff who live out of town and are willing to stay and be available for at least one shift or more a day.'

He glared down at her. She still wasn't used to looking up at men and he was almost intimidating when he was annoyed. Almost. But she didn't like even a fraction of that feeling. Cate walked around her desk and sat down where she felt more in control. For some reason she liked the desk between them. 'Take a seat.'

He was still glaring at her. 'So I'm to sleep in my office? Is that correct?' He almost growled as he perched on the edge of her desk exactly where she'd been sitting. She wondered if the desk was still warm and the thought caused an uncomfortable tension in her stomach. This was ridiculous. He was here to complain.

Cate tilted her head. 'That's right. As the nurse manager will be in hers. And goodness knows where I'll sleep.' The man was behaving like a spoiled baby, and impatience tinged her voice. 'As someone who, I assume, spent some time as an intern during your medical training, surely you've roughed it before between shifts.'

His expression hardened for a moment then cleared. 'Oh, I've done my time in Emergency and roughed it to get some sleep. But I'm older and wiser now and would have preferred not to have had the choice made for me.' His eyes lightened. She couldn't see what she'd said to restore his good humour but maybe he didn't hold grudges. Good. She hated grudge-holders.

He picked up a pen from her desk and started to doodle on her notepad. Without his jacket, the overhead light gave a sheen to the swell of muscles in his arms. Quite impressive they were, too. Amber had said he was a nicely packaged calculator.

When he spoke she jumped. 'So. You're not going home either?'

She glanced away as she realised she'd been staring and tried to marshal her thoughts. Going home. Right. 'I doubt I'd get through, and if I did I wouldn't get back. Most of the bridges upriver are flooded so some roads downriver will close about twelve hours later. Hopefully the rain up at Point Lookout, that's our main catchment area, will stop and all this will be over in a day or so.' Since when did she babble? Cate snapped her mouth shut.

Noah swung his leg and his thigh muscles bulged and relaxed under the fine material of his trousers. Bulged and relaxed, bulged and relaxed, and hypnotised her. She restrained the urge to shift her chair further back, as if he were invading her space. There was some sort of aversion-attraction thing going on here and it needed to stop right now.

Then, when he smiled at her, she couldn't help

but smile back until she realised what she was doing. What was she doing? She was not going to become obsessed with this man.

This was a man who worshipped the dollar more than his Hippocratic oath. He would return to the city after the downgrade of Riverbank Hospital. She needed to remember she had loyal staff like Stella Moore willing to be cut off from her family to ensure the hospital was covered during the crisis. Cate looked away from him.

He looked at her quizzically. 'Now what's made you frown?'

'You don't want to know,' she said, and looked back at him with her lips compressed. 'Is there anything else I can do for you, Dr Masters? I have to get on with my work.'

'Damn. The ice maiden is back.' He dropped the pen on the desk and stood up. 'Let's call a truce, at least until after the rain stops. If you call me Noah, I'll go off and leave you alone quite happily.'

Cate considered the first part of his request and was surprised how much she wanted to stop fighting with him. It looked like this flood drama was going to continue for a few days and it would be more sensible if the two of them worked harmoniously. Or at least tried to keep every discussion away from being based on who was going to win.

She didn't quite meet his eyes. 'As for the truce, I'll give it a go, but if I disagree you'll know about it.'

He laughed. 'I never dreamed of anything less. And calling me Noah?'

She shook her head. 'I'd prefer to keep things professional, if it's all the same to you.' His face became more serious as he stood up, and this time his tone contained no laughter. 'Then I'll settle for Mr Masters. I prefer not to be called "Doctor".'

When he left the office she stared at the empty space where he'd been and considered his parting comment. Why did he dislike being called a doctor? Why had he given up practising medicine? There was a story here. Maybe he had a good reason. Then the phone rang. She glanced at the clock. It was almost teatime. She did have work to do and thinking about Noah Masters wasn't getting it done.

When Stella Moore and the resident failed to turn up for the night shift, Cate chewed her bottom lip. She'd tried the resident's mobile phone but there was no answer. Evening staff had agreed to stay back until further notice but most of them had already been rostered for the next morning and they needed their rest.

An hour after they were due, an ambulance pulled up outside Emergency with the missing pair inside. Stella's cheek was cut and Dr James was scratched, bruised and had suffered minor head injuries. Thankfully, with rest, they'd be fine. But the tree they'd hit had blown Cate's night shift staffing out of the water.

Relieved that neither was hurt badly, Cate left the

evening staff to treat their injuries while she assessed her options.

Noah Masters could sort the medical part. Militantly she knocked at his office door but her battle plan hadn't included Noah opening the door half-dressed.

'Yes?' He wore his lack of clothing like a night at the opera. Cate stared and suddenly the oxygen content in the room fell below the usual twenty-one per cent.

Noah's voice was impatient. 'You knocked, Sister Forrest?'

Cate blinked and tried to stay focused on Noah's expression and the warmth of a blush embarrassed her even further. This was ridiculous. She must be more tired than she'd thought. Her eyes travelled down and she wrenched her gaze away from what seemed like acres of firmly muscled chest and a sprinkling of dark springy hair—hair that curled out of sight into his unbuckled trousers—and she bit her lip. Compared to her previews of what she now saw as Brett's pigeon chest, she was impressed.

Just when she thought she had her brain back in gear he confused her again.

'Why aren't you off duty? Don't you know how to delegate?' His voice was clipped and the exasperation in it jolted her out of her sensual haze quicker than anything else could have.

'I don't have the luxury,' she snapped back. 'Delegation is more your angle.'

His eyes narrowed at her response. I've annoyed him now, she thought. Good. The problem needed a fix. She glanced at her watch. The evening staff needed to get to bed.

'Well, come in.' He stood back to allow her past him into the office and the momentum of the moment carried her through the door and dumped her in the middle of the room. His trundle bed was pushed up against the wall and the door shut behind her with a click. Cate turned to face him and realised it was a very crowded room and most of it seemed to be filled with Noah Masters.

Exasperated and half-naked, Noah glowered at her and Cate moistened suddenly dry lips and tried to remember why she was here. Thankfully, her thought processes came sluggishly to life. Staffing.

Cate cleared her throat. 'The night emergency team have been involved in an accident and we need to find replacement staff for this shift...' Noah walked across the room to lift his shirt from the chair back and Cate's voice trailed off.

He looked up and caught and held her gaze. Noah shrugged his way into the sleeves slowly as if staring at her had slowed his fingers. Cate couldn't help but stare back. There was something disturbingly intimate in the way he was so steadily arranging his clothes in front of her. The muscles in his shoulders and chest rippled as he lifted his arm to slide it through the sleeve, and Cate's breath lodged somewhere deep in her chest. This man affected her *way* more than he should, especially when she knew he was in Riverbank for such a short time. She shook her head in denial of the attraction, and tried to concentrate on the problem she'd come with, and not the way his fingers fastened the buttons on his shirt.

She looked away with a jerk. 'I need to replace the evening staff so they can still work the morning shift. I don't have any more emergency sisters to pull from anywhere, at least until daylight, because I'm not putting more people at risk to drive in this weather.' She glanced back just as Noah tucked his shirt in and tightened his belt. Her gaze flicked away again but then his voice drew it back.

'And you want me to do what?' The words were very soft as he leaned his long fingers on the desk and of all the things she wanted, she wished he'd left the door open the most.

Cate shrugged with a forced nonchalance. 'Find me a doctor to work with and I'll do the nursing part of night shift in Emergency.'

Noah scanned the options in his mind. 'We don't have any spare doctors.' He rubbed the back of his head and Cate only just heard the oath he muttered. He looked up. 'It would take too long to drive another resident in from one of the other hospitals. I suppose I could ask the rescue helicopter to fly in a locum.' He shook his head as he finished the thought. 'But you're right about the risk. The rain is still too heavy for safe flying.'

Cate raised her chin and forced herself to meet

his eyes. 'There is still one doctor left who could work.' He didn't react to her suggestion and she wondered how he'd take it when he realised what she meant. She shrugged again and hammered the option home. 'You do still have your registration, don't you?'

Any subtle awareness of his attraction to Cate, awareness he'd been trying to ignore in the closeness of the room, evaporated at her words. Rumbling lust was driven clear away by the knee-jerk denial of her suggestion.

Him in Emergency? He'd sworn he'd never go into front-line medicine again after Donna had died. And Cate Forrest had no right to push him towards it!

To be fair to the woman, she had no idea how disturbing the idea was to him, that the chance of someone else dying because he couldn't save them scared the life out of him. He just hoped she couldn't see it.

'No.' His voice was firmer than he'd intended but he couldn't help that. The word hung in the air and there was no room for argument. 'Get the evening resident to stay on and I'll arrange a replacement for him in the morning.'

Cate put her hands on her hips. 'He's already done a sixteen-hour shift.'

'I'm the CEO and it's my call—not yours. Thank you, Sister Forrest.' He crossed the room and opened the door for Cate. She glared as she went past but by the time she was halfway up the corridor she couldn't help trying to figure out why he was so adamant. His harsh denial only confirmed her suspicion that there must be a reason he was so determined not to work as doctor.

Noah watched her stride away. He'd thought he'd been safe in administration. Then this had to happen. Of course he still had his registration.

Noah kicked the door shut behind him as he went back into his office. As an administrator, was he willing to run the risk that the overtired resident would be up to handling the night's emergencies as they came in the door? He swore softly under his breath. If anything happened, he'd be morally to blame anyway. He'd have to do the shift himself. Damn the woman.

Noah strapped on his watch and checked his pocket for a pen. He'd be interested to see just how good Sister Forrest was at the clinical stuff.

An hour later Noah had to admit she was good. Very good.

Emergency wasn't overrun with patients. The rain had kept the usual minor illnesses at home but the range of complaints was challenging.

After her initial pleased surprise at his presence, Cate had all the cubicles prioritised and waiting, so that Noah almost felt like a production line worker as he moved between them. It suited him. Emotional involvement was the last thing he needed when doing something he'd sworn never to do again.

Unfortunately, the man in cubicle five was a challenge to ignore. Mr Ellis had been washed into a tree while herding his cattle across a small creek which had turned into a raging torrent. Noah tried to remain impervious to the friendly man who peered intently around the forceps to see the sutures go into his own leg.

'That's not a bad job, you're doin' there, Doc.'

'I'm glad you think so, Mr Ellis,' Noah said dryly, and continued to pull the edges of the deep ragged wound together. 'What time did you say you did this?'

'After lunch. I taped it together but the bandage kept soaking through and the missus said I better get it fixed 'cause I had a lot of work to do in the next couple of days.'

Noah grunted but the silence stretched. He sighed inwardly as he felt compelled to chat with this nice old bloke in spite of his better judgement. 'Did your wife come with you?'

'Nah. She hates boats and our creek's flooded the road. Lucky I parked the car on the other side yesterday. She's at home, putting most of the stuff from the house up into the roof in case the river comes over the verandah.'

Noah tied off the final suture. 'Don't you think it would be more sensible for you both to stay in town until the rain stops?'

The grin died in the weathered face. 'No. We'll ride it out.' The man looked down at the neat line of stitches running across his calf. 'Thanks for that, Doc. Better get going, then.'

'Sister has to dress that first.' Noah turned just as Cate entered with a roll of bandage and a bottle of friar's balsam. He raised his eyebrows.

'Friar's balsam to help keep it waterproof. Mr Ellis will try to keep it dry, won't you, Mr Ellis?' She smiled at the farmer and he grinned back.

'Now, Cate, you know I gotta move them cattle up on high land.'

'Take the bottle with you and mind you put it on a couple of times a day. It will help keep the germs out. You get that leg infected and June will have to do all the work on her own.'

Noah stood up abruptly. 'Which cubicle next, Sister?'

Cate gave him a questioning look. Her answer was even shorter. 'Four.'

As he stepped out of the cubicle he heard her give instructions on when to return for the removal of sutures. Hell! He should have done that, but he was out of practice. He was whistling down the tunnel of medicine and mayhem again and all the old demons were laughing at him. The lack of staffing was bringing it all back, the disbelief and anguish when he'd found out there hadn't been enough doctors to save his own wife. And the guilt. The only thing he'd been thankful for had been that Donna had never known that her own husband was the doctor who hadn't been able to save her. Would she ever have forgiven him?

Noah shook his head and briefly he resented Cate. How had that woman managed to get him here? If he could just get through this one night, he'd make damn sure that Riverbank had more doctors than they could possibly need. And he'd keep his distance from the patients.

In cubicle four an old lady sat stoically on the chair with her hands in her lap. Her face was the map of an interesting life and, white-haired and tiny, she reminded Noah of his grandmother. He could tell she was in pain but nothing obvious stood out. Until she lifted her hand from her lap. Her thumb was red from the base to the swollen tip that stuck out at a bizarre angle.

'Ouch!' Noah pulled a chair gently up beside hers and cradled her wrist in his hand to see the thumb up close. 'I'm Noah Masters, the doctor, and I can see you've dislocated your thumb. It must be very painful.'

When she didn't reply Noah wondered if she was deaf, but then she looked down at the offending digit and shook her head. 'It bloody well hurts.'

Noah bit back a smile. Maybe not so similar to his grandmother. 'We'll take an X-ray, but I'm fairly sure it's not broken, then I'll have to put some local anaesthetic into the base of your thumb and block the nerves. The good news is that all the pain will go away for a while and when I put it back in align-

ment, most of the pain will fade even when the anaesthetic wears off.' He heard Cate enter the cubicle
and she held an X-ray up for him to see. Mrs
Gorse's!

Cate was too efficient and perversely he felt the
prickle of his resentment again. 'Don't doctors have
to order these before you can get them done?' He
knew he was being testy but she was making him
feel threatened with her capability.

'Mrs Gorse came in just as the evening staff were
leaving. I had the resident sign the X-ray request
before he left.' She didn't poke her tongue out but
he had the feeling she'd have liked to. Instead, she
handed him a silver kidney dish with two strengths
of local anaesthetic and a syringe—and left.

The old lady cackled at him and suddenly he
smiled.

'That's better,' she said, and her eyes nearly disappeared into the creases in her face. 'Thought you
had a poker up your bum. You've met your match
in Cate.'

Noah nearly dropped the dish. He looked at her
from under his brows and gestured to her thumb.
'How did you do this?'

She snorted in disgust at herself. 'I was moving
the bull and caught my thumb in his nose ring.'

'I should have known.' Noah waited for the local
anaesthetic to take effect and then manipulated the
joint back into place with a soft click. He glanced
at his watch. 'You moved the bull in the dark?'

She shrugged her unaffected shoulder. 'The river won't wait for the morning.'

She still looked a little like his grandmother even if she didn't sound like her, and again he felt like chatting. 'So where are you going when we get it fixed for you?'

Mrs Gorse looked at Noah as if he were mad. 'I'm goin' home. There's a flood on, you know.'

Cate breezed in. 'You two seem to be getting on well.' She smiled at Noah and then bandaged the old lady's thumb to give some protection. Noah assumed she realised that Mrs Gorse would be back at work as soon as she got home. He stood up and looked down at the two formidable women before he left the room.

So Mrs Gorse reckoned he'd met his match, did she? Now, that sounded more like his grandmother. He stifled the brief moment of loss he always felt when he acknowledged that the woman who had cared for him most of his childhood was gone. Nina Masters had been a strong woman and hadn't hesitated to tell him he was a fool for marrying Donna. She probably would have appreciated Cate. Most likely because she wouldn't have bored her to death like Donna had. He hadn't thought of Nina for ages and now just wasn't the time. He moved to the next cubicle.

A young girl had just been brought in with a raging chest infection and her hacking cough made Noah wince as he shook hands with her worried parents. Cate appeared beside him and handed over the chart with Sylvia's vital signs. Her temperature was elevated and her oxygen saturation was way down from what it should be.

Cate smiled reassuringly at the mother. 'This is Dr Masters, Gladys. Tell him what you told me.'

Gladys squeezed her daughter's hand and looked up with tired eyes. 'She's just not getting better, Doctor. Sylvia's been sick since she had the flu a week ago and tonight I noticed her fingernails were blue. Now she's got pains in her chest when she breathes.'

Noah nodded. 'She's certainly not well. I'd like to listen to your chest, Sylvia.' He looked at Cate who lifted the little girl's jumper up so he could place the stethoscope against her chest. 'How old are you, Sylvia?' Noah asked, and his voice seemed to soothe the frightened child. Cate was glad to see he wasn't trying to freeze the child out, as she'd noticed he'd tried to with the adults.

'I'm six.' The little girl looked at her mother as if to check she was right, and then sat quietly as Noah tapped with his fingers on her chest wall and listened.

'Can you make big breaths in and out? Big as you can, without hurting yourself, please, Sylvia.' Noah leaned forward with his stethoscope and listened to the child's air entry at the front and back of her chest, before standing back.

He spoke to her mother. 'We need to take an

X-ray in the morning, but I think Sylvia has developed early pneumonia on both sides of her lungs. She'll need to stay in hospital for a couple of days, maybe more. Are you able to stay with her?'

Gladys turned to her husband and when he nodded she looked relieved. 'Yes. I can stay tonight at least and then we'll see how the flood goes. Normally it wouldn't be a problem but if the river comes up too far I'll have to help out with the cattle.' She looked pleadingly at Cate. 'But Sylvia has Cate and if I have to leave she'll make sure she's right, won't you, Cate?'

'You know I will, Gladys.' Cate nodded, and ruffled Sylvia's hair. 'Let's hope the rain stops, though.'

Noah frowned but he didn't say anything against more work for Cate. Instead, he spoke to Gladys and her husband. 'Sylvia is a sick little girl. It was a good choice not to leave her any longer. She'll be right in a few days.'

And so the night wore on. He heard tales of past floods from the older people, most of whom seemed to have had a relative almost washed away in the 1949 flood. Apparently the hospital had saved many lives. From the younger folk he heard of the sandbagging operations that were going on through the night. Never having been involved in this sort of crisis before, Noah couldn't help being caught up a little in the air of urgency. The one thing he didn't hear were complaints.

At five a.m., Cate came in with two mugs of coffee and sighed as she sat down beside him at the nurses' station. She looked more tired than he felt and Noah stifled the wave of tenderness she stirred in him. Suddenly, care was needed, or she could easily slip under his guard. He had been through enough with Donna, and the tragic consequences of their marriage, and he just wasn't ready to get involved with another woman. He was beginning to wonder whether the only way to avoid that was to leave town as soon as possible.

Cate sipped her coffee and stifled a yawn. 'Well, that was the last from the backlog. If you want to put your head down, I'll phone your room if anyone comes in who can't wait for the morning staff.'

Typical of her, he thought. She needed the sleep more than he did but already he knew better than to mention it. Noah shook his head and stirred his coffee thoughtfully as he settled back in the chair. What did make this woman tick? 'You seemed to know most of the people that came through. I gather your family have lived here a long time?'

Cate smiled and there was contentment in her voice. 'My great-grandfather settled at Riverbank just after the turn of the last century and we have a lot of relations in the valley. My parents and I work the original farm.'

Her eyes crinkled as she thought of her home, and Noah wondered what it would feel like to have such a network of family and friends surrounding you.

He realised he envied her. 'So you're a real country girl.'

She met his eyes. 'You could say that—yes. Though most of us have it easier here on the coast than those further inland. I really admire the women out west who teach the kids and run the house and the shearing sheds, plus the admin side of farming as a business.'

He realised he was doing what he'd just told himself not to do. He shouldn't be so interested. His voice became more flippant. 'Well, I'm a city boy and mean to stay that way. It would feel strange to know the people you treat all the time. I'm afraid I like a bit of distance from the patients.'

Cate gave him a level look. 'I noticed.' Her voice was dry. 'Is that why you chose to go into administration? Because you don't want to get involved with patients? I heard you used to be a surgeon. You have special skills, Noah, and what you do now seems to me a waste of your training.'

His face closed. 'I've chosen not to work as a practising doctor any more. I can do more good where I am at the present and I believe that. And there are other reasons.'

'Which you're not going to share?' Cate didn't have high hopes but wasn't afraid of asking.

His eyes hardened. 'That's correct. So don't expect me to work in Emergency again.' He smiled but she could tell he meant it as he stood up. 'I think I will go to my office. You can ring me there.'

'Certainly, Doctor.' Cate nodded and watched him leave. Whatever his reasons, they seemed to be very heavy baggage—and she had a strange urge to try and comfort him.

CHAPTER FOUR

Thursday 8 March

THE night finally ended. Cate headed for bed after handing over to the morning casualty staff. She could sleep at least until after lunch, but there was still her afternoon shift as supervisor to cover, which she'd swapped with Amber.

The supervisor's office was in full use through the day but Cate had been offered an empty patient room in Maternity until they needed it. She didn't stir until lunchtime and when she woke to the sound of a baby crying, she turned on the patient's radio beside her bed. The river and bridge level updates were on and her eyes snapped open. All but the last of the upriver bridges were closed. A minor flood on the Macleay, at least, was a reality.

She tossed and punched her pillow but couldn't recapture the dream she'd been enjoying. She was too wide awake. Cate climbed out of bed. If she hurried, she could make sure those who wanted to go home before the last bridge closed made it out in time.

Cate showered the mist from her brain in the private bathroom and smiled to herself as she wondered where Noah was showering. Then she frowned with unease as she remembered her reaction to a half-dressed Noah. And tried not to imagine how devastating he'd be entirely naked...

An hour later, she ran into a bleary-eyed but immaculate Noah in the cafeteria as he made himself a coffee. She couldn't help the small smile about her private thoughts and suddenly all her senses felt amazingly alert.

Cate bounced over to him. 'I've sent the rest of the upriver staff home that wanted to go. The last bridge to cross upriver will be closed in an hour. If it keeps raining they mightn't get home for a week.'

'You should have kept them in case you needed them.' He was obviously not happy about his lack of sleep. He glared at her. 'What are you doing? You don't start until three.'

She grinned. 'I've had five hours. It's enough.'

He grunted but didn't disagree. 'So the flood is closer?'

Cate nodded. 'We've had two hundred and sixty-six millimetres of rainfall up at Point Lookout today. It looks that way.'

He gestured with his hand to ask if she wanted a cup of coffee, but she shook her head. 'No, thanks. By the way, we've had a few calls from women at the outlying villages who are due to have their babies. They're worried they'll be unable to get in when they go into labour. How do you feel about the really overdue women coming in?'

Noah shook his head. 'Don't weaken. We don't

have the staff for extra patients but if they want to come into town they can stay with friends or relatives.'

Cate didn't like the coldness of the answer and she frowned. 'What about the ones that don't have either of those in town?' Cate thought of Michelle and Leif and how their timing had worked for them. Others wouldn't be so fortunate and some could panic. 'I don't want people taking risks either if they feel they have to stay home until the last moment.'

His face hardened. 'Not our problem.' Cate frowned harder but he ignored her. 'If they're that worried they could stay at a motel.' He headed for the table. 'If the worst comes to the worst, I'm sure the state emergency services will get them in here.'

Cate could feel her temper rise as she followed him. Didn't he know these were real people he was talking about? 'That's a big ask for the state emergency services. What about women with fast labours or first babies who don't know how long they have in labour?'

He waited for her to sit down and then did so himself. He shook his head. 'It's not your job to take the worries of the world on your shoulders. If a labouring woman needs to come in and can't, that's when *I'll* worry about her. We are not having pregnant women taking up beds "in case" they go into labour. We might need the beds. Do you understand?'

Cate couldn't believe this guy. How dared he

speak to her like that? She stood up again, aware that she'd better leave before she got herself into real trouble. 'Right' was all she allowed herself and marched away. All the things she should have said ran through her brain as she stomped up the corridor but it had still been a good idea to leave then. She liked her job.

Cate screwed up her nose. Amber would probably wax lyrical about Noah at shift handover. Lately, she seemed to bring Noah Masters into every conversation she could, dwelling on his good points, as if he had any, and today Cate wasn't in the mood. Maybe she could divert Amber with Brett, the only other person Amber seemed to want to talk about.

Noah watched her stomp away and ran his hand through his hair. The first thing he had to do was get a few more doctors to help with staffing. He'd have to check supplies were adequate in the kitchen if the highway shut, and he had an appointment with the SES controller in half an hour. Now, there was another strong woman, he thought with a grin.

He just didn't have time to think about the look of contempt Cate had flung at him before she'd left or why it bothered him. But it did.

Much later in the evening when he caught up with her, he wondered if she'd cooled down. It might be politic to mend fences. It might even be fun. Fun was something he hadn't had much of the last two years, and for some reason Cate seemed to amuse him.

'So how many disasters have you dealt with so far, Sister Forrest?' She was at her desk when he dropped in, ostensibly to look for the nurse manager who hadn't been in her own office.

She looked up but she didn't smile. 'We don't have disasters here, *Mr* Masters. We have moments of unusual interest.'

'Ah.' Noah nodded sagely. He saw that she was alone and decided to put off his search for the nurse manager for a few minutes. He rested his hip on the corner of her desk and looked down on the top of her head. All he could see was blonde-to-the-roots thick hair that sprouted up at him and made him want to brush it to see if it was as silky as it looked. She continued to be absorbed in her paperwork. Or pretended to, he'd wager. He cleared his throat. 'Cate, truce.'

The pen in her hand was thrown down on the desk and she tipped her head back to look at him. It was a nice angle.

'How can I help you, Mr Masters?' Her blue eyes were doing their police siren thing again. At least he didn't bore her.

How could he explain what he was trying to say when he really didn't know himself? 'Cate, I know we can both do our jobs while running a cold war between nursing and administration, but it's much more pleasant to be in sync. As far as our discussion from this afternoon goes, I don't believe we've reached the stage where we need to encourage people to be admitted before they are genuinely required to be here. I need your support on this. We can't let the public abuse our resources at this early stage.'

She pushed her chair back. 'What you don't seem to realise is that the *public* around here don't abuse resources like you seem to expect them to.'

Noah smiled—at least she was talking to him. 'I admit you have more experience with these people but, believe me, if someone needs to come in urgently, we'll get them here.' He put out his hand. 'Truce?'

At least he was listening to her. Cate looked at his hand and thought of the last time she'd touched him. She rolled her fingers in hesitation but then forced herself to shake. His hand was warm and firm and there it was again, a frisson of awareness zapping from his fingers to hers, and Cate pulled her hand away. She glanced at her watch and stood up. 'I'm going for tea.'

'Then I'll come with you.' He was laughing at her. She could either get angry or laugh back. She chose the latter.

The tension eased in the room and they were still smiling when Janet Glover, the nurse manager, came in.

She gave each of them a knowing look. 'Hello, Cate, Mr Masters.' Looking at Noah, she said, 'I want to speak to you.' She glanced around Cate's office. 'Here will do.'

'And, believe it or not, I've been looking for you, Janet.' Noah turned to Cate. 'Sorry. Rain check.'

Cate nodded. 'I'll leave you to it, then.' She was glad he hadn't been able to come, she told herself as she walked towards the cafeteria.

So how did she feel, knowing that Noah had sought her out to pacify her after their words this morning? And, more importantly, why should it matter to him what she thought? She had to admit she was coming to enjoy his company and it certainly couldn't hurt her cause if she could influence him to see the needs of a rural community. Not just in crisis either. With her help, maybe he could grasp the importance of a well-funded and well-staffed community hospital. She could be pipe-dreaming but she'd give it a shot. Of course, that would be the only reason to get to know the man.

Strangely, after a lonely tea, the rest of the shift started to drag and Cate went over to see Sylvia before the little girl went to sleep for the night. The child's mother had had to go home and Cate had promised to come over and say goodnight to Sylvia.

'Hello, darling.' Cate sat on the edge of the bed and Sylvia's little hand crept into hers. 'So poor old Mummy had to leave you to help with the farm?' Cate stroked Sylvia's hair with her other hand as Sylvia nodded.

'Well, the secret is you have to push the buzzer on this cord if you need one of the other nurses to come and sit with you. OK?' The little girl nodded again. 'If you get really sad you can get them to wake me up. I'm sleeping over with the babies at the moment because I can't get home to my mummy either.'

Sylvia's eyes widened. 'Are you going to have a baby, Auntie Cate?'

Ouch. Cate blinked and squeezed Sylvia's hand. 'I hope so. One day. Not for a while, but when I do, I hope I get a lovely little girl like you. Now, I'll tuck you in and we'll both have a good sleep. I'll come and see you when I get up in the morning. OK?'

She dropped a kiss on Sylvia's cheek and the little girl kissed her back. 'Goodnight, Auntie Cate.'

'Goodnight, darling.' Cate hugged her close and felt the warmth of her tiny body snuggled against her. Cate swallowed the lump in her throat as she disentangled Sylvia and tucked her in.

The rest of the shift passed slowly and Cate didn't see Noah again that evening. Odd that she felt like she missed him. She shook herself. Last night's extra shift must be catching up with her! Cate was glad to see the night supervisor come in to relieve her of the keys so she could head to bed. At least she didn't have to get up for the early shift...

Friday 9 March

Cate woke early with nine hours to go until she started work. She lay on her back and stared at the

ceiling as she listened to the local FM station give
out the flood warnings.

Despite the easing of local rainfall, the minor
flood warning was official. Even the garbage men
couldn't do their jobs and residents were requested
to bag and keep refuse out of any sunshine until
collection could be resumed.

It was the little things you didn't think about
when a town became flood-bound, Cate thought.
The next item grabbed her attention when it was
announced that the lower Riverbank floodgates were
to be opened at eleven a.m.

That news gave her a jolt. She'd have to ring her
parents if the phones were still working. As downriver farmers, the land in Cate's family was mostly
river flat and alluvial soil. It would nearly all go
under when the open floodgates took some pressure
off the minor streams. She chewed her lip as she
thought of her frustrated father in his wheelchair and
her mother and Ben having to cope. Maybe she
should have stayed home to help? But it was too
late now.

Any chance of a sleep-in was lost. Even though
she had another quick shift tomorrow, it just wasn't
going to happen.

Before she went over to see Sylvia, she dialled
her parents' number and the phone seemed to ring
for a long time. Finally her brother answered and
Cate heaved a sigh of relief. She would have spent

the whole day worrying if there had been no answer. 'It's me, Cate. How's it going?'

'Cate! Good to hear your voice!' Ben's voice was deeper than she remembered.

A lump lodged in her throat as she realised how much she'd missed him. But she never would understand how he could have left the farm with just Mum and her to run it. What was it with men? Brett had taken a hike when she'd said she wouldn't move to Sydney with him and leave her family in crisis, and Ben had left when they'd most needed him.

Her brother was talking and Cate brought herself back to the present to concentrate on the news.

'The bottom flat's gone and they haven't even opened the floodgates yet. But the cattle are safe. You should see them all around the house! Mum's put a rope up to keep them off the verandah.' Ben's voice was quietly confident that he had it all under control. Her little brother? Ten years younger didn't count once he got to twenty, she supposed. It seemed like she'd always been there to tell him what to do.

She tried to picture him two years older than when she'd last seen him. 'So all the supplies are fine and Dad's OK?'

'Everyone is fine. The house has never been touched in previous floods, so we're hoping we're safe. The water line is still a fair way away at the moment. How's the hospital?'

A picture of Noah filled Cate's mind. 'We'll manage.'

'If they have you in charge they won't have any choice.' They both laughed but Cate was uncomfortably reminded of Amber saying something similar about her need to run things. Was she that bossy? She'd always been a leader but maybe people got sick of being led. She sent her love to her parents and hung up.

After showering, Cate's feeling of disquiet lingered. She visited Sylvia but the little girl had a new admission to talk to now, another girl her own age, also with pneumonia. Cate left them to it and headed for breakfast. Maybe she was hungry. When she entered the cafeteria, Noah was already there. It would be churlish to sit at another table, she told herself, and took her cereal over to stand beside his chair.

'Feel like company?' Her voice was more forlorn than she'd intended.

He glanced up, saw who it was and smiled. 'Feel free.'

He stood up until she'd sat down and this time it gave her a warm feeling in the pit of her stomach that he'd do that for her. Cate couldn't help but smile at him and her uneasiness lifted a little.

'That's better,' he said. 'You looked worried a minute ago. And you shouldn't be worrying until your shift starts at three. Tell Uncle Noah.'

She stirred her muesli and looked across at him, amused. 'You're no relative of mine.'

He shook his head and laughter lines she'd never noticed before creased his eyes. It made him even more attractive, if that were possible. 'I thought you were related to everyone in the valley?'

'Only locals.' She pointed her spoon at him. 'And you're not a local.'

His nod was judicious. 'How do you get to be a local, then?'

She laughed. It was a joke for all newcomers. 'At least twenty years and a few kids born here would help. But even then it usually takes a couple of generations before you're *really* a local.'

'Well, I'm only on the coast for a couple of months. I'll have to live without local status.' He shrugged and Cate felt a little pang of emotion at his words. This was getting ridiculous, she thought. Did she *want* him to stay or something?

'So, tell me what's upset you.' Noah's voice made her turn back.

'How do you know I'm upset?' She stared at him.

He shrugged again. 'I've had more practice with that emotion than seeing you euphoric.'

Cate sniffed. 'So I'm not only bossy, I'm cranky as well.'

It was his turn to frown. 'Someone said you're bossy? You sound tired.' His voice gentled. 'Go back to bed, Cate. I've watched you the last couple of days. You do a great job, you give everything, but you're going to wear yourself out.' He laid his hand over hers for a moment. 'Sure, you're bossy.'

He smiled to take the sting out of it. 'But you have to be. That's what bosses do.'

She must be getting soft in the head because she felt like crying when he'd praised her. Which was ridiculous. She spooned a mouthful of muesli in to distract herself and help push the lump away from her throat. But she could feel his gaze on her and when she looked up he was smiling at her.

His voice was deep and lazy and something inside her responded to it. 'You need to get out and away from here. Want to come for a ride with me down to SES before you start work? I've another appointment with the controller to check out the sandbagging site this morning.'

He was only being kind, but Cate had to admit she liked the fact that he'd asked her. A tad too much, if she was honest. Then there was the thought of getting away for a couple of hours before another tense nine-hour shift. The idea had merit. To hell with it. 'Sounds good. I'd like to.'

'I'll see you in half an hour out the front, then.' He stood up and they both glanced at the time. Noah laughed. 'Do you want to synchronise our watches, Agent 99?' His impersonation was dreadful, but she laughed anyway.

When she met Noah at his car, his eyebrows nearly disappeared into his hair. Cate was dressed in gumboots, cut-off jeans, an oilskin rain jacket and black Akubra hat. The clothes were different but her long brown legs were gorgeous and he tore his eyes away with reluctance. A pair of gardening gloves poked out of her pocket.

'I don't think I've ever seen you look so relaxed,' he said as he opened the door of his car for her.

Cate hesitated before she slid into the plush seat. 'Is that a polite way to say I look like a hobo?' She didn't wait for an answer. 'Nice car. Should I take my gumboots off? Or I could even walk down.' She frowned and gestured to the SES centre, which was plainly visible from the hospital. 'I don't know why you're taking the car anyway.'

'In case it rains and I'm needed back here urgently.' Noah caught her look. 'I'm not lazy—just sensible. Cate Forrest, you are the most forceful woman I have ever met.'

He looked her over and she wasn't sure if it was her imagination that his gaze seemed to linger on her bare legs. 'Why are you dressed like that?'

She threw up her hands in a pose. 'This is what all the best-dressed sandbag-fillers wear!'

He chuckled before turning the key to start the car. 'I suggested an outing—not a second job! Are you really going to fill bags?'

She grinned at his expression. 'The bags need filling and I need the exercise. I've been inside for three shifts, and a couple of hours of physical labour will be good for me.'

Noah could think of a more pleasant way to burn off energy. He shook his head and stamped down his baser instincts. 'You're mad! But I had an idea of that anyway.' He pulled out into River Street. 'So, what do you do on this farm of your parents?'

'Fencing, manage the cattle and horses, maintain the vehicles. All the usual farm stuff.' She shrugged it off.

Noah was intrigued. He'd bet she was good at all that physical labour, too. 'My impression has always been that farming was done by the farmer, not the farmer's daughter.'

Cate shot him a look. 'Don't be sexist. My mum helps as well. Dad manages the business side of the farm now. He was an Australian horseman of the year before his accident landed him in a wheelchair.'

Noah winced in sympathy. 'A horse-riding accident?''

Cate's eyes clouded briefly. 'No. A branch fell on him.' She didn't say any more and Noah didn't want to push it.

The silence stretched and then Noah spoke up. 'Do you have any brothers or sisters or farm helpers?'

Cate stared straight ahead so that he couldn't see her expression. 'One younger brother, who left home a couple of years ago. But he's home for the flood and seems to be doing everything I did. They're managing well.'

He shot a look at her profile. 'You sound surprised. Shouldn't you be happy about that?' He was pulling up at the SES centre and suddenly Cate wanted to get out without answering. She *should* be happy that Ben was coping perfectly without her. She just had to get used to it.

Noah seemed to be able to read her too well for the short time they'd known each other. It might be wise to maintain some distance from him. And remind herself he was here to downgrade her hospital, before leaving again for Sydney.

But she'd decided to worry about that part of his portfolio after the flood. She had to admit the minor crises she'd laid at his door had been sorted quickly and efficiently. He was very good at his job, even if it wasn't the one she thought he should be doing. She lifted the doorhandle and slid out of the car— to safety.

CHAPTER FIVE

THE SES control centre was manned by a dedicated band of volunteers who didn't complain when they were pulled from their beds to attend to some emergency. The sandbaggers were even more eclectic. Each mound of sand had its own work party of bag-fillers and another group retrieved and loaded the bags onto a truck to transport to one of the levee banks.

Cate pulled on her gloves and joined one of the smaller gangs, eager for something to divert her mind from Noah. The others in the gang, most of whom she knew, looked up with tired smiles but didn't pause in their shovelling.

An hour later, Noah walked over to where Cate toiled happily. She didn't see him approach and he stood for a moment and watched her easily shovel the sand into the bag held by one of the other women. To Noah, there was something carelessly sensual in the way she dug and lifted and emptied the sand in a rhythmic sequence. A sheen of perspiration on her well-shaped arms testified to her efforts. The stacks of filled bags proved the collection of people were a team.

He couldn't think of any of the women he knew

in Sydney who would consider doing this to help out. But the controller had told him that between the different sandbag operations there were nearly a hundred women and two hundred men, not usual volunteers to the SES but all helping during the flood for the common good.

It was becoming a worry that he admired Cate more every time he saw another facet of her personality. She looked up and saw him and her smile drew him to her side.

He cleared his throat. 'I have to go back. Janet Glover has an emergency.'

Cate leaned on her shovel for a moment and wiped her forehead. Tiny grains of sand trailed across her face. 'I'll walk up later.'

'Close your eyes.' Noah leaned forward and brushed the streak of sand off her face and immediately regretted it as he felt the smooth softness of her skin. Now he would feel her under his fingers for the rest of the day. What was it about this woman that penetrated the shell he'd thought impervious?

He looked hard into her face as he said, 'I'll see you this afternoon, then.'

Cate watched Noah stride back to his car. What had he been looking at? She really hoped he hadn't heard her small gasp as his fingers had brushed her face. She flushed as she imagined those fingers sending electricity through her whole body... What was wrong with her?

Cate glanced around at the other volunteers in her

gang, hoping they hadn't noticed her distraction. Luckily, the two grandmothers, four teenage boys and half-dozen men were too absorbed in their work. Soon they'd need another mound of sand. Apparently there were bagging gangs on both sides of the traffic bridge and along the levees as well.

By lunchtime, Cate was feeling much better and, having helped a bit, was ready to go back to the hospital. Out of the corner of her eye, she noticed that one of the grandmothers, Ida Matthews, had paused in her shovelling to rub her foot. 'Mongrel thing,' Ida muttered, and shifted her body weight to get comfortable.

Cate handed her shovel to another young lad who had just arrived. 'Have mine. I have to go.' She moved across to the elderly woman. 'Sore foot, Ida?'

Ida put her foot down gingerly. 'I stood on a nail in the garden a couple of days ago and it's giving me trouble today.'

'How are you for tetanus coverage?' Cate bent down and slid the gumboot off Ida's foot. The sole where the nail had gone in was hot and red. 'I'll hitch us a ride back to the hospital and you'd better see a doctor in Emergency about that foot. I don't like the look of it.' She smiled at Ida, who was a known chatterbox. 'It would be terrible if your jaw locked up from tetanus.'

Ida smiled back tiredly and shrugged. 'If you

think I should. I didn't like to take their time if they're busy.'

Noah should hear this, Cate thought wryly. 'That's what they're there for. Let's go.'

Cate left Ida with the emergency staff and took herself off for a much-needed shower and some lunch. There was still an hour before work—time to phone her parents to see how they were faring as the water rose.

Her father answered the phone. 'Hi, Dad. It's me. How are you going down there?'

'Hello, Cate, love. We're fine but I'm glad we got out of dairy cattle and into beef. At least we don't have to milk cows in a dairy a foot under water. The road is cut off and the milk trucks can't get in next door. Poor devil will have to throw his milk out until they can pick it up. But it could be worse.'

Cate smiled at the expression. Even in hospital when her parents had found out about his paraplegia, they'd both said, 'It could be worse.' 'How's Mum?'

'Your mother is wonderful, as always. She's enjoying having Ben home and she's taking photos to show you. She's not happy about the influx of snakes, though. They're heading for high ground and I guess the house paddock is it. Ben had a black snake try to climb into the saddle with him yesterday. It was the funniest thing.'

Cate joined her father's laughter as she imagined it. 'Rather him than me.'

William Forrest's voice became more serious.

'How are they going in town? What have you been doing?'

'I'm fine. I went to SES this morning to help fill sandbags before work. The town is gearing up for the water to top the levees.'

'Well, let's hope it doesn't. That will be hardship for a lot of people.' His voice held the memories of previous floods.

She could hear the sound of a calf lowing in the background and tried to imagine the cattle all around the house. Cate wished she could transport herself home just to see that they were all OK. To use her parents' expression, it could be worse. At least she had the phone. She glanced at her watch. 'I'd better go. Love to all. Bye, Dad.'

'One thing before you go, love. I've forgotten his name. The CEO at the hospital. How're things going with him?'

Cate felt the heat flood up her cheeks. What had her mother said? Her brain froze and she said the first thing that came into her head. 'His name's Noah Masters and he's a bit infuriating at times. But we're getting on fine, Dad.'

'That's not the name. Fellow by the name of Beamish. That's who I meant. How's his leg?'

Cate cringed and felt like an idiot. 'Oh. He's comfortable, Dad. Mr Beamish will be in for a few more weeks yet but he's on the mend.'

'Right. That's good. Bye, love,' he said, and hung up.

Cate put the receiver down slowly. She was fixated on Noah Masters and it had to stop. Cate stared out of the window and wished she were home. Surrounded by water, it would be even safer. She tried to picture how the farm must look to drive the image of Noah out of her brain. The sun was shining outside the hospital today, maybe that was what was making it all the harder to imagine her home.

When Cate entered the supervisor's office, Amber and Noah were standing beside the radio for the two o'clock news. For some weird reason, she didn't like seeing the two of them so close together. She closed her eyes for a moment and promised to beat herself up about that later. She moved over to stand beside them to listen.

A moderate flood warning had now been issued for Riverbank township with a peak at four p.m. Schools and preschools were being evacuated and the water would soon creep over the highway between Seven Oaks and Frederickton.

After switching the radio off, Cate and Noah listened as Amber gave an abbreviated report of the status of the hospital.

'I won't be able to come into work on Monday if the schools are still closed,' Amber said.

Cate shrugged. She couldn't get home anyway, she thought and handed Amber her umbrella. 'Try for childcare on Tuesday, maybe.' Unconsciously she copied Noah's dictum. 'We'll worry about it if it happens.'

Amber turned for the door. 'By the way, Brett arrived to be with his mother. I had lunch with him and he's very upset.'

Cate looked up with a questioning look but Amber was halfway out of the door to pick up her daughter.

Noah allowed himself to enjoy just seeing Cate again. The frown that she'd worn earlier had gone and she seemed renewed by the exercise of the morning. Most people would be still in their beds— but not Cate. 'You look better' was all he said.

'Clothes maketh the woman,' she quipped as she moved around the desk to answer the phone.

'I didn't mean the clothes.' He waved and left the room. Cate stared after him. So what had he meant? She picked up the receiver—the call was from Emergency. It was Stella Moore.

'What are you doing back at work already, Stella?'

'Well, I can't get home so I may as well do what I came to do.'

Cate could hear a baby crying in the background. 'How's the head?'

'Fine. You brought in Ida this morning, is that right?'

'Yes. I was wondering what happened with her. How is she?'

'Starting to show signs of tetanus poisoning,' she answered bluntly. 'She's on antibiotics but we need to send her to Sydney for possible hyperbariac oxygen treatment at North Shore. We're up to our eyes with patients out here. Could you do me a favour and arrange it all and let Ida's family know? She'll have to go by helicopter.'

'No problem. Look after yourself and ring me if you need a break.' Cate finished writing down the information and pulled out the phone book.

'Thanks,' Stella said, and hung up.

It took Cate an hour to sort out the transfer of Ida Matthews, photocopy her admission notes and get her family in with some belongings for Ida to take with her.

A further hour later, Cate hugged the woman as she was transferred to the helicopter that waited at the hospital helipad.

'We'll be thinking of you, Ida. See you when you get back.' Cate helped the wardsman pull the stretcher away from the helicopter door.

Ida nodded forlornly, too sick to speak, and then the door was shut.

Cate and the wardsman stood for a moment with their hands over their ears as they watched the rotors start. At least the rain had stayed away but the cloud cover was thick and seemingly impenetrable. Cate was glad she wasn't the one flying. After her father's accident her mother had gone with him in the helicopter and Cate had spent the next few hours positive the helicopter would crash. She hated flying.

Back inside the hospital, Cate made her way to Iris Dwyer's room. A once-familiar figure stood beside her bed and Cate hesitated in the doorway. But it was too late—he'd seen her.

Brett came swiftly towards her and enveloped her in a smothering hug. 'Hello, Catie-pie.' For a moment it was hauntingly familiar but then it irked her.

How had she ever thought that pet name was sweet? 'Hello, Brett.' Cate untangled his arms from around her neck and, as he leaned forward to kiss her, she turned her cheek in the nick of time. Cate studied his angular features and couldn't help but compare him to Noah. It was no contest. Poor Brett.

She stepped to the side and around him into the room. Thank goodness she wasn't as flustered as she'd thought she'd be. Time eased a lot of awkwardness.

'When did you get here, Brett? How's your mother?' Cate's voice was almost a whisper as she moved to stroke Iris's hand.

Brett frowned at Cate's avoidance of him and followed her to the bed. Iris appeared to be sleeping. 'I had a rough trip up in the car. The highway's almost covered in water, and I just managed to get through.' He looked at his mother and sadness welled in his eyes as he answered the second half of Cate's question. 'How do you think she is? She's dying!'

Cate winced at his lack of tact at his mother's bedside. She didn't say that hearing was the last sense to go because they both knew it. She sighed. 'Have you been to the farm yet?'

He looked aghast. 'Why would I go to the farm?'

Cate shook her head. 'The animals? To see how it's faring with the rain? To reassure your mother that everything is all right maybe?'

He shrugged. 'Mum will have arranged for people to do that. I want to stay with her.'

Cate did believe that. He loved his mother and was a kind man at heart. He didn't see that he could be incredibly selfish because his mother had always arranged everything for him. 'So how have you been? I know they've had a problem trying to contact you about your mother's illness.'

'That wasn't my fault.' He sounded petulant and Cate sighed again. How had she ever considered marrying this man?

But he'd been different when he'd first come back from Sydney. Perhaps being several years older than her had helped. She'd never had time for men before Brett and it had been head-turning stuff to be treated like a precious woman for once. She'd never actually figured out what it had been he'd wanted from her, unless it had been to have something that no one else in town had had—herself. But he hadn't even got that.

She'd had this vision of herself and Iris on the farm, caring for Brett and hopefully their children. For a while there it had looked like working. Brett had been loving and had seemed happy for Cate to organise their wedding. Then, out of the blue, he'd mentioned he'd applied for a position at a Sydney practice and what a good doctor's wife Cate would make. What he'd really wanted had been Cate's undivided attention in a role she hadn't been interested in. Cate's world had come crashing down and she'd realised that she'd fallen in love with the dream more than the man.

After Cate's brother had left home and she'd said she'd stay to help on her parents' farm, Brett had realised that she wasn't going to totally devote herself to him. So he'd broken off the engagement and had gone to Sydney without her.

Cate had been left with a guilty relief. She should never have agreed to marry him when she hadn't truly loved him. And here he was back, at his mother's deathbed, treating Cate as if he'd never been away. How typical.

Cate needed some space from Brett and her own guilt. She looked down at Iris as she slept. 'I have to get back to work, Brett. Give my love to Iris when she wakes.'

He nodded. 'I'll come and find you after six o'clock. We'll have tea together in the cafeteria. Just like old times.'

Cate closed her eyes for a second. 'Not quite like old times, Brett,' she said dryly, 'but if I'm not busy I'll have tea with you.' She straightened the cover on Iris's bed and stroked her arm. 'Bye, Iris,' she said softly, and nodded at Brett as she left.

'Later,' she heard him say as she walked away. Cate rubbed her temples and glanced at her watch.

She needed to check that everyone had tea relief organised and she wondered where Noah was.

Now, there was a totally different scenario. Imagine being married to Noah! That would be a different marriage to one with Brett. The woman who married Noah would have to submit to him being the boss. There was no way Cate would tolerate submission to any man. A sudden vision of a home with Noah and a tribe of strong-willed little children curved her lips before she realised what she was thinking.

Blimey. What *was* she thinking? Cate started to walk even faster than her usual pace as if to get away from the startling picture she'd painted.

Her pager beeped and she headed for Emergency. Diversion was at hand. Hopefully the place would be wall to wall with people.

When Cate entered the department, Stella looked calm as usual amidst the chaos. 'I need to clear some of these patients. A heavy vehicle was swept off the causeway. We've got the three passengers, who clung to trees in the middle of the river for an hour. Two have broken bones and all of them have hypothermia. Which ward can we put them in? I can't see any free beds on my admission sheet.'

Cate picked up the phone. 'I'll try to send them to Maternity. Two more mothers were discharged today from there. We have a three-bed room over there that's empty and we'll just have to hope the storms don't bring on the babies.'

She spoke quickly to the maternity staff and hung up. 'That's fine. They'll come over and transfer them to save you the work. What else have you got?'

'I've a resident with a migraine who's trying to work, two men with chest pain and a waiting room full of cuts and bruises, plus the first few cases of gastro.'

Cate picked up the phone again. 'Noah?' She didn't realise it was the first time she'd called him Noah without thinking. 'It's Cate here. We need another resident. One of the ones in Emergency has a migraine and the place is snowed under. OK. Ring me back, I'm in Emergency.'

Stella raised her eyebrows. 'Good luck,' she mouthed, and moved away to attend to a small child who had lost his mother in the mêlée.

Cate turned back to the desk while she waited, and checked the notes of the new admissions. They could go straight to Maternity when the staff arrived to take them.

She chewed her lip. The gastroenteritis was a worry. If the water kept coming up, the risk of an outbreak would increase. She shrugged. That was Noah's worry.

When she turned around, the subject of her thoughts was standing there with a stethoscope around his neck.

CHAPTER SIX

NOAH looked so solid and reassuring, but Cate was surprised to see him. 'I thought you weren't going to work in Emergency ever again?'

Noah didn't smile. 'One last time and not for long. I've already arranged for two medical residents to arrive from Newcastle. They'll be here in an hour and I'll work out here until they arrive.' His eyes pierced her. 'Do you want me to get extra nursing staff from another hospital before the highway is cut off?'

'No.' She couldn't provide doctors but the nurses all knew their responsibilities. 'Our own staff are capable of managing a local problem, thank you. I've had calls from staff making themselves available if I need them.'

He looked around at the ordered chaos. 'Well, use them. Get extra staff when you need them.'

Cate's eyes widened in surprise. 'Hallelujah. What about the budget?' She shot a startled look at him. 'Who *are* you? What have you done with Dr Masters?'

'Very funny.' He bared his teeth and Cate smiled.

'I thought it was.' She watched his eyes darken. Then she realised it offended him that she thought so little of him. What a joke. She thought too damn much of him. That was the problem. Still, it was safer for her own peace of mind if he didn't see she was fighting a burning attraction.

Cate held up her hands. 'Fine. Thank you. Stella will be pleased to have extra staff.'

'Since when have you waited for permission?'

She became serious. 'To my distress, sometimes I do. The happy medium is hard to find. But I don't have to worry about that today. I'll just say I did what I was told.'

As she turned towards her office, she heard him mutter, 'I wish.'

It was six o'clock before Cate had the staffing as she wanted it. When she looked up, Brett was lounging at the door to her office.

'Ready for tea?' he queried, and she could tell he expected her to come right away.

He struck a pose and handed her a rose, probably stolen from the hospital garden, she thought. She closed her eyes as she sniffed it. The scent reminded her of other times that he'd brought her flowers.

She dropped the rose on the desk and stood up. 'OK. Let's go. But my pager will probably ring half a dozen times so there's no use getting cranky with it.'

'I never get cranky,' he said. Brett slipped his arm through hers and clamped it to his side before she could pull away.

Petulant, not cranky, she corrected herself, and he

could be very sweet. But she still thanked her stars she hadn't tied herself to this man-child for the rest of her life.

When they entered the cafeteria, Noah was there. Not sure why she should feel so relieved to have already disentangled her arm before they'd gone in, she still felt strange, with Brett by her side and Noah looking on. Which was ridiculous. Especially when Noah didn't appear at all interested.

Cate chose a table by themselves and deliberately she directed Brett into a chair so that she had her back to Noah. Unfortunately her neck itched the whole time she sat there.

Brett talked enthusiastically about his junior partnership in the Sydney practice but half of Cate's concentration wondered if Noah had left.

When Noah appeared at her shoulder she jumped, and Brett looked surprised at the intrusion. Reluctantly Cate introduced them.

'Brett, this is Mr Masters. He's the area CEO. Mr Masters, Dr Brett Dwyer.'

Brett held out his hand. 'Mr Masters.' They shook hands and Brett winced at the pressure. He flexed his fingers and then looked fondly at Cate. 'What Cate didn't say is that I'm her fiancé.'

Someone dropped a tray of crockery at the same time as Cate said, 'Was. Past tense, Brett.' Hell. Cate doubted if Noah heard her as he was looking at Brett, but she couldn't justify repeating it. She didn't know why it bothered her what Noah thought, but she felt better when she kicked Brett under the table. Cate directed her voice at Noah. 'Brett's mother is terminally ill in Medical.'

Noah nodded. 'I remember. Mrs Dwyer. I'm sorry about your mother's illness, Dr Dwyer.' He nodded at them both. 'I'll leave you to your conversation. Good evening.'

Brett stared after him. 'Seems OK for a CEO. Not a bad job, that. Maybe I should look into it.'

Cate couldn't help but laugh and that was the sound Noah heard as he left the cafeteria.

Noah needed to breathe the outside air. Urgently. It had been a long day and he was tired. He'd been hoping to catch Cate at teatime but the last thing he'd expected had been for her to be with another man, let alone her fiancé.

Though she had said, 'Past tense.'

Still, she must like the guy if she was eating with him. And Dwyer must want her back if he was willing to say they were still engaged. Noah pushed open the door to the garden.

Funny, she'd never mentioned a fiancé before. She'd always struck Noah as brutally honest. Obviously he hadn't asked the right questions.

So what was that news to him? Noah ducked under a tree branch and slapped the trunk as he walked past.

At the very least it was disconcerting to find himself upset by it. She *had* crept under his skin. What Noah had seen in Cate had amazed him. A woman as smart and determined as he was and someone who understood that sometimes hard decisions had to be made. As long as it wasn't to do with her hospital, of course!

True, she was totally different to the type of woman he'd usually been attracted to, but much more exciting. He'd been enjoying the challenge. The more he came to know her, the more he liked what he saw, and appreciated that she could be the perfect partner for him.

Which was probably what Dwyer thought, too!

Later that evening, before she went to bed, Cate listened to the latest radio bulletin. The meteorological bureau had issued a projected peak height for Riverbank at six-point-five metres at noon on Saturday. Which meant the highway would be cut off on both sides of town and there would be a flood of water in the main street and through the business district some time during the next morning.

Noah had told her that the army and navy were sending helicopters to pick up stranded families and those needing assistance. Food drops were being organised and extra ambulance personnel were on their way from Newcastle. Cate shook her head as the announcer confirmed that the town had been officially declared a disaster zone.

All these years of hearing about the floods and now she was here for one. She prayed that no lives would be lost. That was the most important thing.

But only two things were certain in this weather—
the hospital was built on a hill so it couldn't get
flooded, and tomorrow would be another busy day.

Saturday 10 March

Cate woke to the sound of rain on the roof. A few
minutes later, the thump of helicopter rotors vibrated
through the air and she lay and listened like a be-
mused child. She swung her legs out of bed and
stood up to stretch the kinks out of her back.

When Cate went in for breakfast at seven, Noah
looked in fine form. He sat opposite a very crumpled
Brett and she struggled to keep a straight face. Considering the similarities of their profession, she
couldn't think of two more different men.

When she went over to the table Noah stood up.
Brett must have thought he was leaving because he
looked confused when Noah sat down again when
she did.

She swallowed a hiccup of laughter and pretended
not to notice. 'Good morning, Noah.' She turned to
her ex-fiancé. 'Good morning, Brett. How's your
mother?'

Brett was obviously pleased to have Cate's attention and he edged closer to her. 'She woke a couple
of times during the night but her condition is much
the same as yesterday. I slept in the chair beside
her bed.'

'I was just saying he looked like it,' Noah commented.

'That was kind of you, Noah.' Cate kept her shoulder turned towards Brett. 'Iris must have been pleased to have you there. But I'm sure she'd think you should go to her house for a sleep today.' Her voice softened. 'I can phone you if she needs you.'

Brett visibly drooped. 'I am tired. Maybe you could come out to the farm this afternoon after work? We could have tea there before coming back here.'

Noah shook his head at Cate. 'Sorry, Dwyer, but I've booked Cate to come for a ride in the SES boat this afternoon. The controller especially asked for her. And then we have to discuss what we find in relation to health factors.'

Cate nearly choked on a mouthful of muesli. When Noah offered to pat her back she declined with a glare. Brett just looked more confused.

What was Noah playing at? Cate glanced at her watch. It was later than she'd thought. She'd have to go soon. 'You look exhausted, Brett. I have to go to work and you should be in bed. Drive carefully. At least the farm is on the flood-free route.'

He nodded. 'You will wake me if there's any change or even just to say hello.' Brett looked so forlorn Cate dropped a sisterly kiss on his head before he got up to leave.

'I'll let you know, don't worry.'

As Brett sauntered out of earshot Cate narrowed

her eyes at Noah. 'I've never heard so much rubbish in my life. Why would anyone from the SES ask for me?'

'Angela likes you. Actually, she asked me and I asked for you. I thought it would be a good chance for you to get out for an hour or so. Then you can fill sandbags or whatever afterwards.'

'So why do you want me…' she tapped her chest '…to come?'

Noah shrugged and pretended to whine. Unfortunately he sounded very much like Brett. 'You're my only friend here?'

Cate's head lifted. 'That's cruel. His mother is dying.'

Noah looked disgusted. 'I have sympathy for his mother, but her son is a dweeb. How could you be engaged to that?' He shook his head in disbelief.

Cate glared at him. 'He treated me with respect.' She tilted her head defiantly. Noah stared implacably back.

'You deserve respect.' His voice was clipped. 'Give me another reason.' His face said he couldn't think of one good enough.

Cate couldn't meet his eyes. 'I thought I could love him.'

Noah snorted. 'Came to your senses, eh?'

How dared he? 'This is none of your business.' Cate tapped her fork. 'And I have work to do.'

Noah held her gaze for a long moment before saying firmly, 'Fine. Remember you have an appointment at four o'clock.' He strolled out of the cafeteria before she could say anything further.

At four o'clock, Noah opened the door of his car for Cate. This time she wore three-quarter-length black jeans and a red-checked shirt knotted at the waist. She had red sandshoes on and no socks, and he loved her in that black cowboy hat.

'Do you always have footwear appropriate to the occasion?' he said.

'I try.' She glanced down at his leather shoes and bit her lip. She couldn't wait to see him wade to the flood boat in them.

He caught her eye and smiled sardonically back. 'My gumboots are in the back so you can stop gloating.'

She inclined her head in appreciation of his forethought. 'So how does a city boy have gumboots in the back?'

Noah stared ahead at the road. 'Is that a riddle or a question?'

A smile tugged at the side of her mouth. She knew what he was doing. 'You're stalling for time while you think about something else, aren't you?'

He glanced across at her and his face was serious. 'Doesn't it amaze you that we can be so in sync?' His eyes returned to the road. 'We understand each other too well sometimes.'

Cate frowned and tried to make sense of his comment. Then the sight ahead diverted her. The car had to backtrack to the highest cross streets to get to where the SES boat waited at the flooded road. Cate's eyes widened. She hadn't been born in 1963 for the last big flood and it was bizarre to see the main road to the centre of town disappear under the water.

The flood boat was waiting, pulled up on the bitumen. Noah parked his car back on a slight rise opposite the ambulance station.

They pulled on lifejackets and one of the other men shoved their boat off so that they were propelled slowly down the main road in a metre of water. Angela Norton, the controller, an enthusiastic thirty-year-old, looked more tired than she usually did. She pointed out the waterfall over the levee, with water streaming across a lake that used to be playing fields.

'The Kemp Street levee overtopped at midday and the water came through the center of town pretty fast after that. A metre of water in less than an hour caught a few out. Most emptied what they could from the shops overnight,' Angela said.

The boat turned into Stuart Street for an eerie float through silent streets. Some shopfronts were filled halfway up the window height with water. Lounges bobbed up and down and everywhere strange objects floated out of context past their bow. People waved from the top stories of buildings and everywhere, despite the brown water covering familiar landmarks, the people they saw were cheerful enough.

Noah shook his head. 'It would turn me off, having a shop in a flood zone,' he said.

Angela nodded. 'There's a lot of work to fix it. But the water will go down.' She steered the boat around a submerged car. 'One of the oldtimers used to say, ''You can always come back with your livestock after the water has gone, but always go early and shift in daylight hours, not in the dark.'' Luckily, we had a fair idea she'd go over today.'

A television news helicopter thumped noisily overhead, no doubt taking their photos for the nightly news. When it had moved on, Noah asked about the other helicopters they'd heard were coming.

Angela nodded. 'We've got a few. There's a Chinook that landed at South West Rocks in bad weather and decided to stay. Plus the three Seahawks from the navy, six from the army and an Iroquois aircraft. The Chinook's gone to Bellbrook as there are a hundred stranded people to move from there.'

Noah winced at the numbers. 'So those people go to the local high school refuge centre? Do you have enough food and bedding?'

'We'll have over two hundred refugees there tonight. The church ladies are buttering up a storm of sandwiches at the showground and others are packing food drops. A lot of bedding and clothes have been donated from the families in town and hopefully it will only be for a few days. There's a queue of trucks both sides of town that were on their way between Sydney and Brisbane. They can't get through but at least the hospital and people on the west side of town have the train line to deliver food supplies.'

Cate could see Noah was impressed. She was conscious of a lump of pride in her chest at the smiling faces around her. Most were willing to bide their time and get on with life when mother nature had finished with them. The rest of the boat ride passed mostly in silence.

Noah was still quiet as they drove back towards the hospital and Cate pondered where she could be the most help for the next couple of hours.

Those victims cut off from home struck the closest chord with Cate. 'Drop me at the high school and I'll have a scout around to see how they're coping.'

Noah turned to look at her. 'Don't you ever stop?'

'Why? I might find a health risk. Besides, I can't sit on my hands until tomorrow's shift.'

Noah shrugged and turned the car. 'Fine. I'll come with you. The hospital can page me if they want me.'

By the time they'd spent two hours at the high school, finding necessities for people and arranging for others to contact relatives, Noah and Cate had heard more hair-raising stories than they could possibly remember. They'd listened to plenty of praise for the volunteers who had saved what they could from the water and some of the stories were harrowing. Times present and past when the access to the hospital had been a deciding factor in saving someone's life seemed to strike Noah the most. Cate planned to take full advantage of it. Hopefully, Noah would see more 'town need' than dollar signs when he returned to being an administrator.

Noah agreed to drop two of the stranded women off at the showground on his way back to the hospital to help with the food preparation. Cate suggested they go in to say hello.

Inside the old weatherboard building she knew every face, because whenever there was a crisis—be it flood, fire or man-made disaster—these were the people who always turned up. There were a lot of elderly men and women—arthritis and stiff legs didn't bar these people from buttering enough to feed the multitude—Noah smiled, shook hands and congratulated people on their effort. Cate felt a warm glow spread through her as she watched him.

Back in the car, again Noah didn't say much and Cate stared out of the window, praying he was receptive to the needs of the community.

It was close to eight o'clock when they pulled up at the hospital and Noah turned off the engine. Cate had leaned to open her door before she'd realised he hadn't moved. She sat back in the dark and waited for him to speak.

'That was pretty incredible,' he said, and the emotion in his voice was testimony to his reaction. He turned to face her and a beam from a streetlight illuminated the strong planes of his face. 'It's the human spirit thing, isn't it? I think I lost it two years ago when my wife died and now this flood has given me a touch of it back. Thanks for sharing it with me, Cate.' He leaned across and kissed her cheek before reaching to open her door.

'Goodnight, Noah.'

Cate climbed out and leaned on the door to look back in.

Suddenly, it seemed neither of them were ready to end the evening and Noah heard himself say, 'I'll park the car but it's still early. Are you up for a game of pool in the nurses' home?'

Cate hesitated. She'd probably spent too much time in Noah's company than was good for her. But the competitive demon inside her couldn't resist the challenge. Maybe this was a chance for her to win at least one round against him. 'One game. Then I'm going to bed. We country people go to bed early, you know.' She shut the door and stood back.

Cate watched him start up the car again. She stroked her cheek where he'd kissed her. So Noah was a widower? More clues as to the nature of his baggage and more intriguing questions she didn't know the answers to. Cate kicked a stone as she turned away and it skidded ahead of her and disappeared into a shadow. A bit like the pieces of Noah's life that she wondered about.

Cate entered through Emergency and for a change

it seemed quite civilised. Stella was on the evening shift again and lifted her hand in greeting as Cate walked through. They should compare hours worked at the end of this, Cate thought with a wry smile.

The hospital corridors were quiet as she continued until she came to the children's ward. She dropped in to see Sylvia but the little girl was sound asleep. Cate wrote a quick note and folded it like a card for Sylvia to find when she woke up. She propped it on top of her black hat so Sylvia would see it and know Cate had been by if she woke in the night. Then she slipped out of the back door.

Cate followed the path beside the nurses' quarters to the old laundry which had been converted into a games room. Most of the equipment had been donated and two junior nurses were having a rowdy game of pool when she pushed open the door. They were just finishing up, with only the black ball left on the table. Cate grinned at them and plonked a coin onto the edge of the coin-operated pool table to claim the next use, then wandered over to battle the pinball machine until Noah arrived.

A few minutes later, Noah nodded to the nurses playing pool. Their girlish voices made him feel like Methuselah and he wondered when he'd become so old. He stepped over to stand behind Cate as she gyrated at the end of a prehistoric pinball machine and suddenly, ridiculously, he felt sixteen again.

Her thigh pressed against the metal as she bumped it with her pelvis every now and then to direct the ball, and he watched, fascinated, as she threw her whole concentration into the game. For the first time in his life he wished he'd been born as an arcade machine. The thought made him smile.

The fact that Cate had barely noticed his arrival didn't escape Noah. She was immersed in the game. The silver ball flew around the course and her long fingers tapped madly at the flippers to block the ball from sinking.

He hadn't seen one of these machines for a long time but obviously Cate was no stranger to it. She was good, a lot better than he'd be, and he grinned at her intense concentration as she gripped her bottom lip with her teeth in determination.

The digital counter flew into the hundred thousands in response to her unerring aim at the targets and she muttered to herself as the last ball eluded her and disappeared down the centre hole. She'd just missed out on a free game.

'Pretty good score, Sister Forrest.' When she turned and grinned up at him he felt like dropping a kiss on those pink lips of hers but he hesitated a moment too long. She turned back to the machine to calculate her score. This wasn't the place, anyway, he consoled himself. Maybe coming here hadn't been a good idea.

Across the room, the young nurses finished up their game and waved goodbye. Now that Cate's machine had stopped ringing and beeping, when the door shut behind the girls with a whoosh, it was silent in the room.

Cate flexed her fingers and patted the machine then she turned to the pool table. Her eyes sparkled blue and challenging and he couldn't help the answering smile that tugged at his lips. She vibrated with energy and he felt the tension zapping between them. He wondered if she did.

Lately he hadn't found her so easy to read. Sometimes he wondered if she felt anything at all when he was around. It was very disconcerting.

Cate hopped from foot to foot like a champion tennis player. 'Let's see how good you are at pool, then, Mr Masters.' She lifted her favourite cue from the wall-mounted rack. 'One game. Choose your weapon.'

Noah perused the rack of cues and decided on a nicely weighted mid-length. So, she thought she could beat him, did she? He hid his smile. 'Set 'em up.' He reached for the triangular rack and placed it on the table as Cate inserted the money and collected up the balls from the drop-tray. 'Would you like to make a small wager on the outcome?' His voice was nonchalant.

Cate was chalking her cue and she looked up equally innocently. 'Sure. Whoever loses…pays for the game.' She threw him the chalk. 'You break.'

Their eyes met across the table as he dusted the cue tip with the chalk, and his fingers slowed. Suddenly there was a lot of heat in that look and he was intrigued that it was Cate who looked away first. Maybe she wasn't as oblivious to him as he'd thought. He stared down at the more than adequately chalked cue tip and dragged his mind back to the game. The woman was addling his brains!

Cate was quiet as he broke the stack, and with more fluke than skill the number ten spun off into the side pocket. 'Looks like I'm after the big ones, which is only fair seeing as I'm taller.'

Cate nodded but her smile didn't reach her eyes. He saw that she was actually planning her next move and he grinned at her competitiveness. He shot again but the ball missed the pocket and she brushed past him as she moved around the table to line up her target so that she was opposite him.

When she bent over the table he had to avert his eyes from the straining buttons on her shirt and the soft swell of her breasts as her neckline opened. He'd thought a game of pool would be fun before turning in for the night but he was afraid this could be more in the way of torture. Clunk went the ball.

She slid past him to lean in front of him and he stepped back out of her way to admire the view as she bent low over the table and the short jeans tightened across her bottom. A bit like his jeans were tightening. At this rate he'd be spending the night in a cold shower. He gritted his teeth. Clunk.

Noah averted his eyes again as Cate leaned even further down on the table, then came back to the present with the sound of another ball thudding home into a pocket. Startled, he saw that she'd sunk all her balls and only the black eight ball and his four coloured ones were left on the table. Thankfully, the black ball bounced harmlessly off the cushion away from the pocket.

He moistened his lips and loosened the tension in his shoulders. 'Nice of you to give me a shot.' His voice sounded incredibly normal, and Noah narrowed his eyes to concentrate.

She smiled up at him. 'You'll only get the one chance.'

She thought she had him and Noah felt like playing dangerously. 'Then let's up the ante.' Noah lined up his shot. 'Loser pays for another day's game as well.' He paused, then added, 'And the winner gets a kiss.'

Cate sent a startled glance across at him, but didn't meet his eyes. She was in no mood to lose. 'You can bet what you like because I'm going to win and I don't want a kiss.'

Noah just smiled and proceeded to coldly sink his four balls and then the black.

Cate winced ruefully. 'Damn. Well done, smart alec. Obviously I shouldn't have let you off the hook.' Cate shook his hand. 'Enjoy your win. You can live without the kiss.'

Noah inclined his head. 'Gracious Cate. I'll look forward to another game when your shifts allow it.'

He gestured at the clock. 'Are you sure you don't want another game now?'

Cate was backing away and shook her head. It wasn't the thought of the game that unsettled her, rather the atmosphere that was thick between them. She was very aware that the sounds everywhere else had quietened for the night. Then there was the fact that the hairs on her arms rose whenever he brushed past.

It had been building all day and there was that kiss he'd dropped on her cheek in the car that she hadn't wanted to dwell on, as well as the startling news he'd dropped just prior to that.

For the last twenty minutes she'd worked hard to block out his presence while she played, but it was as if someone had thrown the switch of her immunity and now she could feel every glance like a caress. It was time to get out of there. Quickly. 'I'm for bed. I'm on an early shift in the morning.'

'Goodnight, sweet Cate.' He walked towards her and her heart thumped as he drew closer. She wondered if he was going to ask for his kiss and couldn't help but wonder what it would feel like to be kissed—properly—by Noah.

He paused in front of her and in the end he just reached out to take her cue. She looked at the floor in case he saw the disappointment in her eyes and told herself she was glad that he hadn't demanded his prize. She was safe.

He replaced their cues in the rack and strolled over to the pinball machine. 'I think I'll stay for a while. I need to practise on this thing if I don't want to get beaten.'

Cate forced a smile and turned for the door. Just before she went through, he stopped her.

'One minute, Cate.' She didn't turn, couldn't turn, and she heard his footsteps come towards her across the room. It felt like someone had superglued her feet to the floor and her heart thumped so loudly she felt it vibrate through her skin. The air seemed to have been sucked from the room and her respiration rate increased to accommodate that and the fluttering discomfort in her belly. Brett had never had her in this state. Brett had never had her in any state.

Noah stopped behind her, and she still didn't turn. But she could feel his breath on the back of her neck and then his hand on her shoulder. The warmth seeped through her shirt and into her skin as he turned her to face him. She didn't even think of resisting.

'It's only fair I get one kiss.' His eyes darkened to black Sambucca, and his finger lifted to stroke her cheek. Cate's heart thumped even faster at that single touch and then he cradled her chin firmly until his lips lowered to hers.

His lips were warm and firm as they brushed against hers, then his mouth took possession. Cate closed her eyes and let him have his way. Because she couldn't lie to herself any more. She wanted to be kissed by Noah. Needed to find out what it was like to be kissed by this man. To be held against him, to breathe him in and be thoroughly kissed. Just once before he left.

And it was nothing like she'd expected. Her few previous kisses disappeared in a purple haze of pressure and taste and heat between Noah's mouth and hers. She floated and soared and whimpered with delight as Noah stamped his mark on her mouth and her heart, and her body flattened against him. She finally realised why she'd never lost her head with Brett. Because it hadn't been like this.

And then he stopped. His hand loosened on her chin until, stroking gently, his fingers released her. His mouth drew back with a few last nibbles and he stepped back. Cate almost stumbled and he caught her shoulder briefly to steady her before he turned her back to face towards the door.

'Goodnight, Cate.' His voice seemed to come from a long way away and Cate flicked a glance over her shoulder at the closed expression on his face. She drew a deep breath, not caring if he heard it, and closed her eyes for a moment. Then she turned and looked him straight in the face. 'Goodnight, Noah.'

The door slammed behind her as she left and she winced. Outside, the night air washed over her face and she gulped in the night scents and the coolness. Her skin tingled in the cold air and the fact that every nerve ending seemed to be more alive than ever before amazed her. She tried to work out what had just happened, but couldn't.

She felt like jumping in her car and speeding down the road to escape for a while and sort out her feelings. But the only open road led to Brett and she wasn't going there.

Which led to another awkward question. Why hadn't she been lost to all reason with Brett like she had with Noah? Scary stuff. She'd almost married Brett.

A few minutes later Cate was back in her room. She showered and crawled into bed and stared at the ceiling. Her mind swung towards Noah. She shied away from the kiss in the games room and focused on his comment in the car. The comment he hadn't explained. The one about losing his wife.

How had she died? Two years wasn't very long to get over grief like that. And why was she, Cate, so upset by the news that Noah had been married before? It took her a long time to get to sleep.

CHAPTER SEVEN

Sunday 11 March

IRIS DWYER died at five o'clock on Sunday morning—without fuss and with a smile on her face. Early morning was a time a lot of souls slipped away and strangely enough when a lot of babies came into the world, too.

Brett had asked the night supervisor to wake Cate and she had been there when his mother had breathed her last. He'd clung to Cate and she'd comforted him as best she could until finally Brett wiped his eyes. 'What am I going to do without her?'

Cate stroked his hair. 'She looked very peaceful, Brett, and her faith was strong. And you'll be fine. Have a few days at the farm to say goodbye and go back to your practice in Sydney. It's where you belong.'

'Come with me, Cate. We could be happy.' His mother's blue eyes implored her.

Cate squeezed his hand. 'You're upset, Brett. You know I'm not leaving here.'

'What about if *he* asks you? Noah Masters. Will you go then?' He pulled his hand away.

Where had that come from and why would Brett ask such a question? Was it that obvious that she admired Noah? Cate bit her lip. She hoped not. There was no future in it and she didn't need to be a further object of pity by the people she knew.

Cate shook her head. 'You're out of line, Brett. But, no, I've no wish to leave Riverbank.' She pushed him gently towards the door. 'Go home to your mother's house, *your* house, and have a rest. I'll see you later today.' She hugged him once. 'Your mother was a wonderful woman. I loved Iris, too. Goodnight.'

Cate went back to bed but she couldn't sleep. Iris's death brought the mortality of human life close to home and it really made Cate think about the choices she'd made in life and love. Was the threat of Noah taking over her life, that loss of control, worth denying herself the pleasure she knew she could find in Noah's arms?

Cate resigned herself to her sleepless state and rose again. Maybe a walk would help. By the time she was dressed, the east was lit with a pre-dawn glow, and she felt calmer.

She ambled down to the Euroka lookout where the river rushed past like an angry brown anaconda, tumbling logs and branches in its wake. When the sun came up, she saw a cow float past on its side and she hoped it was alive.

There was a chance it could be. Yesterday she'd heard about a cow that had been washed through the floodgates, floated on its side for seven miles parallel to the beach and then turned up at Crescent

Head where it had climbed out over the footbridge and ambled away. The newspaper had christened it Bubbles.

Life was strange like that.

Maybe that was what she liked about hospitals, and Maternity in particular—the strange ups and downs but always the continuity of life. Would she have to leave it all behind to follow Noah?

She glanced at her watch. It was nearly time to go to work. It had been a long week and she was due for a couple of days off tomorrow. But if Amber couldn't come in, Cate guessed she might as well stay on for another shift and have extra days off after the flood crisis was over. But she was tired. And confused. Before Noah had come along she hadn't been like that.

Just prior to going on duty, Cate rang her parents. She sighed with relief when Leanore answered the phone. 'Hi, Mum. It's me.' Cate felt her throat close over and swallowed a couple of times before she could talk.

'What's wrong, love?' Her mother's voice was warm and comforting as only a mother's could be.

Cate sniffed. 'Iris Dwyer died this morning. And I needed to tell you that I love you.'

'I love you, too, darling. I'm sorry about Iris. Was Brett there?'

'Yes. He'll go back to Sydney in a few days.' Cate brushed the tears away from her eyes.

There was silence at the other end of the phone

for a moment as her mother thought about the news. 'You must be tired. It's been a long week for you, too.'

'I'm OK. How's the farm and everyone?' Normality at home seemed so far away.

'We're fine. The water is still about ten metres from the house but we took turns at keeping watch last night in case it sneaked up quickly. The cows have ruined my garden but we haven't lost any stock yet, which is wonderful. The only nuisance is that the electricity failed yesterday and we're eating the perishables like mad before they go off. When you see us we'll probably be all ten kilos heavier.'

They both laughed and Cate silently thanked her mother for being there. The hospital's power had been fine so it was probably only the outlying farms that had been affected. Another thing to be grateful for.

'I'd better go. I'll probably give you a ring tomorrow. Love to everyone. Bye, Mum.'

'Bye, darling.'

Cate replaced the receiver and let her shoulders droop. Everything was OK. She'd just plod on for another couple of days and then she could go home.

Her thoughts turned to Noah. Would he be in the cafeteria this morning? How would she feel when she saw him? Did he think last night's kiss had been a token for the winner of a game of pool or had it meant more to him, too? Now he'd managed to land her in unfamiliar territory again.

The lift in her spirits, when she saw him, was proof of how much his company was beginning to mean. Was it still less than a week since he'd come? The shock of that awareness made her tone more abrupt than she'd intended.

Her plate hit the table with a tiny thump. 'Every time I come here you seem to be here. You spend a lot of time in the cafeteria.'

He raised his eyebrows at her. 'Good morning to you, Cate Forrest. That statement is very similar to one you made the first day I met you.' His brown eyes captured hers. 'You really do think I'm a lightweight, don't you?'

Cate sat down opposite him. His broad shoulders strained against his shirt as he leaned back in the chair and his relaxed demeanour belied his ability to know what was going on at any given moment.

Her heart ached as she realised how much this man could come to mean to her. She had to stop this. He'd leave soon. 'No. I don't think you're a lightweight. As much as I hate to admit it, I think you're very good at your job. I don't know anyone who could have done it better. I just wish you were on my side.'

He leaned across and squeezed her hand. 'Did you ever consider that I might be?'

If only she could believe that, because there was another matter that had come up just before she'd come in to breakfast. 'Good. Because Susie Ryan, a first-time mum from Gladstone, rang me just now and I want to bring her in before she goes into labour.'

He pulled his hand back as if it had been snapped by a mousetrap. His voice was deadly quiet. 'You don't give up, do you? I said, no pre-labours and no unnecessary admissions. This hospital is not a motel. Surely you can see we have to keep as many free beds as possible?'

Cate tried to reason with him. 'My instinct tells me this woman needs to come in.'

Noah was adamant. 'When you get an order from a doctor she can come.' They glared at each other and all conversation was halted as they entered into some kind of staring match.

'Right.' Cate pushed her cereal plate away and stood up. 'My fault for mentioning it. Hopefully you won't still be sitting here at lunchtime.'

She should have just arranged for Susie to come in. That was what you got for trusting the enemy. She walked quickly away before she said something she'd really regret and his voice drifted after her.

'Pleasure working with you.'

You have no idea, buster.

Adrenaline carried Cate through most of the morning and she ignored her growing headache.

Noah came into her office before lunch with Janet Glover, the nurse manager.

His voice was clipped, and he spoke to a spot just over Cate's head. 'We need you to make a list of possible extra staff to call in an emergency. There's a chance we could have a severe outbreak of gastroenteritis in one of the outlying towns. The sewerage system has flooded and we have the chance of raw sewage in the flooded streets.'

Two could play at this game, she thought as she spoke to the plant behind him. 'Why not evacuate the town until the danger is past?'

'Because most of them won't leave.' Noah saved a hard look for Cate. 'Country people are stubborn.'

Janet looked amused at the tension between Noah and Cate. She drew them back to the matter at hand when she added her opinion. 'We're setting up public information leaflets to explain the risks and outline the precautions for the townspeople to take, so hopefully the situation won't arise. But Mr Masters seems to think that you may not have the staff resources if you need them. Should we have other hospitals on standby?'

Cate ignored Noah and spoke to the nurse manager. 'I've been inundated with calls from off-duty staff willing to come if we can pick them up. The SES have no problem with that, as long as there aren't any other crises at the time, so I'd say we're well covered.'

'Thank you, Sister.' Janet looked smugly at Noah. 'Does that satisfy you, Mr Masters?'

Noah nodded at Cate and they both left. Cate crossed her fingers that they wouldn't need the staff. Gastro was a horrible illness and the numbers could swell before you knew it.

The rest of the shift was routine until just before shift handover to the evening staff. Her pregnant friend, Susie Ryan, rang again.

'Cate?'

'Yes, Susie? You all right?' Cate saved what she'd been doing on the computer and listened.

'I think so but I hope I'm not getting paranoid. I thought I'd run it by you.'

Cate frowned. Susie sounded agitated. 'Great idea. Go ahead.' Cate sat back in the chair.

'I've got pressure down below but no pains.' Susie spoke fast, as if she wanted to get it out without sounding too much like a fool. 'I haven't had any pains like they said I'd get, but everything feels different down there. What should I do?'

Cate's mind ran through the possibilities, the most likely being early labour. 'Listen, Suse. Because it's your first baby it's probably OK. But I'm off duty in less than an hour. I'll see if I can get a lift with one of the flood boats up to your house and come for a visit. Would that be OK?'

'That would be great. Pete's away, trying to save the oysters.'

Cate winced. 'Floods and oysters don't mix, do they?'

'No. It looks like we'll lose ninety per cent of them but Pete told me to worry about the baby, not the oysters.'

Cate had to smile. 'He's a good man. I won't be long.'

Susie didn't seem to want to hang up. 'It's funny. I'm getting nervous. The last hour I've been feeling really strange.'

'I understand. I'll see you soon. Ring me if you need me earlier and we'll get a helicopter to pick you up.'

Thankfully, the evening supervisor was early and as soon as possible Cate dashed over to Maternity to grab an emergency delivery pack. She slipped the tiny packet into the big pocket of her windcheater. She was sure she wouldn't need it but felt slightly better with its presence.

Cate drove her utility to the spot where she and Noah had embarked from yesterday. As she'd arranged earlier, a yellow SES boat was waiting with a burly teenager at the engine.

The two of them took off in a wave of brown water. 'I'm Paul,' the young fellow said. 'Normally we have two boats if we're going into the main river, but the other boat got called away. You OK with that, Sister?'

Paul seemed quite confident and Cate nodded. They drove past the semi-submerged town and into the main river, keeping towards the less turbulent side. The sun shone off the brown water and the sky was filled with fluffy white clouds. It was really quite beautiful as they steered with the current down the river. Cate could see it would be much more exciting coming back against the flow as she watched Paul avoid the floating debris. The sun was shining off the water and flocks of water egrets circled overhead as they watched hungrily for fish.

It took about half an hour to get to Susie's farm and, amazingly, the water came to about a hundred feet of the house. The grass looked strange to Cate, and Paul handed her a can of insect repellent. She looked at him and he pointed to the ground. The grass and trees near her were a mass of spiders of all different sizes as they scrambled for dry ground. She shuddered and sprayed her legs with the repellent before stepping out.

Susie had come out to the verandah and Cate hurried up the steps to hug her.

Cate took one look at the fear in her friend's face and made her decision. She'd worry about Noah later. Susie was dressed in a skirt and blouse and her rounded belly poked out in front like a beach ball. The fabric tightened over the bulge every time she moved.

'You're coming back with me. You should be happy at this time, not scared witless. Can you get a message to Pete to let him know you're going in?'

Susie's relief shone in her eyes. 'I said I might go back if you said it was all right. Pete was happy about that. He'll ring as soon as he saves any oysters he can. My bag's packed.'

'Good girl.' Cate stepped into the house and lifted the bulging bag beside the door. 'Let's go. I'm not impressed with your watchdog spiders.'

Susie shivered. 'The snakes are worse. We must have five varieties hiding under the house.'

Both women were glad to get to the boat. Cate helped Susie with her lifejacket and then they sat together in the middle of the boat. There was a slight breeze and the first part of the ride was peaceful as they crossed over submerged fences and paddocks towards the river. Paul radioed Control to say they were heading back with precious cargo.

Noah was there and he couldn't believe he'd heard right. Cate hadn't told him she'd planned this and if he hadn't been down here at the control centre he wouldn't have known. He flexed his fingers. He visualised the river they'd only briefly skirted yesterday and he could almost feel the force of the water in his imagination. Wasn't that woman afraid of anything? Well, he bloody well was. He'd strangle her. As long as she didn't kill herself.

Back on the river, Cate had found something to fear. The boat had just made it into the main stream when the engine spluttered twice and died. Even though it had been in the background all the time, the sudden silence from the motor accentuated the grumbling roar of the rushing river.

Cate's hold on Susie's hand tightened as they listened to Paul abuse the boat as he pulled the cord to restart the engine. Strangely, Cate had a sudden vivid image of Noah and the thought steadied her. Susie clutched her stomach.

Paul fiddled with the fuel line and swore again as

the nose of the boat swung back the way they'd come. As their forward speed dropped off, Susie moaned. The boat rocked and was swept away with the river and out towards the middle of the flow. The hull thunked as floating logs jostled with it in the wash.

When Noah heard the distress call come through on the radio, his stomach dropped. He met the eyes of Angela and the worry in her face was enough to chill his blood.

'Get me on the helicopter that's going after them.'

Angela was calm in the crisis and contacted the nearest army helicopter. She glanced up at Noah. 'There's one at the hospital helipad now. I'll ask them to wait for you.'

Noah strode to his car and the engine roared as he accelerated up the hill to the hospital. He drove the wrong way up the one-way lane and parked beside the helipad just as the rotors started up.

'What's happening?' he shouted as he ducked his head to climb in.

The pilot ignored him as they took off and the navigator gestured for him to come closer. 'We've got them on radio and are talking Paul through repriming the engine. It's their best shot.'

Noah couldn't believe it. 'Why doesn't he know how to do that without help?'

'He does. But it's better to talk it through in moments of crisis.' The navigator pressed his earphone closer to his ear. 'He's got it going and the boat is turning.'

Noah sagged back on the bench seat until he saw the navigator press the earphone to his ear again. 'Copy that,' he said, and wiped his face. 'Hell. At least we have a doctor on the chopper.'

'What?' Noah almost shouted.

'The patient's water's broken and it looks like the baby's coming.' The soldiers in the cabin exchanged looks.

A baby Noah could deal with. Cate's boat without power on the river was more of a problem. 'Get them to the edge of the river. And get us down there.'

The next few minutes passed in a blur for Noah as he stared out the window and willed Cate's boat to find somewhere safe to land. The river flashed below him and the flotsam and debris all looked like Cate to Noah.

Finally their quarry stopped and the helicopter settled a little further back from the edge of the fast-flowing water.

Noah was the first out, his face like a thunder-cloud. He pulled Cate from the boat, hugged her once and then thrust her aside to gather up the pregnant woman in his arms.

'Let's go,' he shouted at Cate as she stood, stunned, and stared at him.

Cate couldn't believe it was Noah. She'd never been so glad to see anyone in her life. She had to admit she'd been scared. Birth was natural but boats and cold winds were not normal for newborn babies and a dead motor in flood waters was just too much.

Now she had to get into the helicopter and she hated flying. Her hand started to shake and she nearly dropped Susie's bag. She couldn't get in, but Noah was already inside with the mother-to-be—and Susie needed her.

Cate felt like throwing up as she was pulled inside and with the thump of rotors above them it all swam in front of her eyes. They were finally in the air. Cate had hold of Susie's hand again but she wasn't sure for whose comfort it was.

Susie moaned and closed her eyes. The baby's birth was very close and Cate blocked out the thought that they were hundreds of feet up in the air skimming across a river that would love to gobble them up.

'It's OK now, Susie.' She poured as much reassurance into her smile as possible.

Susie's eyes sprang open. 'That was pretty wild, Cate.'

Cate squeezed her hand. 'Guess whose baby is going to be a real rural survivor?'

'It's coming now.' Susie's eyes widened and her breath shortened. 'How can that be when I haven't had any pains?'

'Your baby is doing this his or her way.' Cate smiled. 'Every now and then that's how it works.

But you've known all day it's coming so that's like labour.'

Susie's hand tightened and she spoke through gritted teeth. 'I have to push.'

'Well, push, Suse.' Cate knew that nothing would stop the birth of Susie's baby and all she could do was make it seem as natural as possible in a noisy helicopter surrounded by five men, four dressed in camouflage. She smiled at Noah with the knowledge that he was there to help. Susie and her baby would be fine.

'Let's get organised.' She reassured Susie before reaching down under the blankets to remove her underwear.

She heard Noah ask for a medical kit and some towels and she remembered the kit in her pocket. She pulled the plastic bag off it and spread the wrapping open to make a tiny clean area. Inside were a plastic kidney dish, a pair of scissors, two plastic cord clamps and a pair of gloves. You really didn't need much to have a baby, she thought whimsically.

Susie moaned and Cate soothed her as she settled the blanket back against itself to reveal Susie's legs and the tiny sliver of baby's head as it peeped through his mother's perineum. Cate donned her gloves and waited for Susie's baby to arrive.

Slowly more head appeared as Susie opened like a flower, her labia spreading as the dark-haired child unflexed its head and then rotated it into the world. Cate rested her hands gently on each side of the baby's head and checked carefully for cord around the neck. When she didn't find any, they waited for the next contraction. Suddenly, with a gentle rush, the baby slid into Cate's hands. Damp and slippery, the little girl mewled at the faces around her.

'Look, Susie. What have you got?' Noah's voice was deep and soft.

Susie opened her eyes and gazed in awe at her daughter. 'It's a girl.' Cate wiped the baby with a towel and clamped and cut the shiny purple lifeline as Susie unbuttoned her shirt so her daughter could lie inside next to her skin and keep warm.

Ten minutes later they made a strange procession as they came through the doors of Maternity, a soldier pushing one end of the trolley and Noah the other. Susie and her baby were buried under a mound of army blankets. The baby didn't cry at all.

Noah left them at the door to Maternity when his pager beeped, and Cate took over his end of the trolley. His eyes pierced Cate's and his voice was implacable. 'Ring me when you're finished.'

She found herself simply nodding.

Surprisingly quickly, Susie was settled into bed with baby Chloe in a cot beside her. Cate wrote up Chloe's birth information in her mother's medical records and the birth register. When that was done, Cate laid down her borrowed pen, rested her head in her hands for a moment and thanked God it had all turned out well.

She massaged her forehead. Could she have done

anything differently? Had her association with Noah affected her ability to trust her own instincts? Could she have known without hindsight that it would have been safer to fly Susie out of there? Or had it been a chain of circumstances that had just happened? She'd never know.

The other disturbing fact was that her thoughts had gone to Noah in her neediest hour, and he was a man on a mission who was just passing through. How was she going to feel when he went back to Sydney?

Noah pushed open the maternity door. He hadn't been able to wait. His fear while the boat carrying Cate had tossed at the mercy of the swollen river had ripped his heart out. A picture of Cate, lifeless on some muddy bank, sat in his brain like a spectre.

He was furious. With Cate for putting herself at risk. With himself for not listening when she'd wanted the woman to come in. With SES for having a boat with an engine that had died and even with baby Chloe for deciding to be born at such a dangerous time. And all of that anger was ridiculous and he knew it. Just couldn't help it.

Because he'd nearly lost someone who matched him in every way. Someone who filled him with the knowledge that he was alive and living life to the full. And the more he learnt about her, the more he cared. And the really scary thing was that he knew he'd be happy to keep learning for the rest of his life.

But she should never have gone out on that boat alone, and he was going to tear a piece off her so that she would never do anything so dangerous again.

Then he saw her, her head in her hands as she sat at the desk in the office. She looked forlorn and was probably beating herself up for everything not turning out perfectly. Suddenly all the anger seeped out of him—he just needed to hold her.

Noah shut the door and then stepped up behind her and rested his hand on her shoulder until she turned.

'Stand up,' he said, and for once she did what he asked without questioning. He turned her to face him and gently pulled her into his arms to hold her close.

She resisted and he shushed her and then she was soft and pliant against him. He cradled her head against his cheek and reassured himself that she was solid and warm and safe in his arms. His Cate. That subtle perfume she wore wove a tighter spell around his heart and he closed his eyes for a moment.

'We have to talk.' His voice was low and deep and it sent shivers across Cate's neck.

His arms felt strong and comforting around her and she'd never felt so warm and safe and feminine. She'd always thought her femininity would make her weak but she felt stronger with his strength around her.

When his lips met hers she understood that kisses

could be many things. This was different and wholesome and awesome and Noah. Cate felt welded to him with heat and homecoming. He crushed her against him and she gloried in his strength. Her fingers spread up and over his shoulders and she held him against her as if to confirm this was where she belonged. It all felt so right.

Insistently, the phone rang beside them on the desk and reluctantly they broke apart. Cate felt renewed and smiled softly and intimately at Noah as she picked up the phone.

CHAPTER EIGHT

IT WAS Brett and the mood shattered into a million jagged pieces. 'I thought I'd find you there. I'm in the cafeteria. Come and have tea with me.'

It was the last thing Cate wanted to do but she'd promised she'd see him today. It seemed days since Iris had passed away and yet it had only been this morning. She hesitated and Noah raised his eyebrows in question. The warmth in his eyes scattered her wits and she turned away from him to answer. 'Give me five minutes,' she said into the phone. 'I'll meet you there. Bye.'

'Who was that?' His brows had snapped together.

It was his tone that did it. He expected to be obeyed. Cate frowned. 'Have you designated yourself as my keeper now?'

'I said we need to talk.' His voice was low but inflexible.

'Perhaps,' she said more cautiously as she realised he'd planned to railroad her and she'd nearly crumbled. 'Perhaps not.' Her decision was made. 'I have to go.'

He caught her hand as she brushed past him and she stopped. Cate looked down at where he held her until his fingers loosened and he dropped her wrist. 'Very sensible' was all she said, and she walked away.

Noah took a deep breath as he watched her disappear up the corridor. She was stubborn and he'd been a fool. He couldn't force her to listen to him and he certainly couldn't expect her to feel the same as he did.

All he was sure of was that today, terrified he would lose her, he'd realised without a doubt that he loved Cate. Why had he tried to steamroller her just now? He'd make up for it next time, unless she did something to make him forget.

Brett stood up when Cate appeared at the table beside him. She admitted wryly to herself that he'd always been a fast learner. 'How are you, Brett?' They sat down together and he leaned across and rested his forehead against hers.

'Sad. And lonely.' His voice was mournful and she sighed. She was beginning to wonder if she'd spent the whole year engaged to him exhaling in frustration.

Cate concentrated on consoling him but the weariness inside her was hard to hide. 'You'll always be sad your mum isn't here to talk to. She loved you so much, and she'll watch over you. That's not my job, Brett. Go back to Sydney. Some wonderful woman one day will capture your heart and you'll settle down and have a family and be someone's dad. You'll recapture the essence of your parents when that time comes.'

He squeezed her hand. 'Are you sure it can't be you?'

Cate shook her head. 'I've changed, Brett. I'll never be that woman. But you will always be special to me.' Cate didn't have the strength or the inclination for this. Iris had been her friend, too, and the day had been too much. And then there was Noah. She could feel exhausted tears hovering very close. 'Look after yourself.' She stood up. 'I have to go.'

Brett gestured to a salad he'd ordered for her. 'What about your tea?'

'You have it. I'm not hungry.' She was sure she'd choke if she ate anything.

He stood up as well. 'Someone else can have it. Walk me to my car, then. Amber's invited me to tea if you were too busy.' Cate nodded. He wasn't going to make a scene, and in relief she even let him take her arm as they went.

In his office, Noah turned away from the window as they walked across the car park. He didn't need to see this. After a few minutes, when he thought he'd be safe, he turned back in time to see Cate give Brett a brief kiss. He swore softly under his breath and turned away again. That had been stupid. Served him right. They said that curiosity killed the cat but he'd have preferred to kill Dwyer.

Cate was exhausted. There had been a cold moment on the river when she'd thought all of them in the boat could lose their lives. And then the helicopter ride had terrified her. She should be thankful to Susie for taking her mind off the flight while she'd had her baby.

Life was funny like that. Things that you'd considered important didn't mean as much if something more momentous was taking place. Soon Cate would walk past Noah's office on the way to her room in Maternity. That kiss they'd shared had only confused her more. Why couldn't she have felt like that with Brett and not Noah? She felt hollow inside and wondered if the ward had any medicinal brandy. She needed a drink and a shower. Or maybe she just needed Noah?

Her feet paused of their own accord and she considered going in to face him. But what would she say when she didn't know what she wanted? Cate resumed walking. She felt emotionally bankrupt and her feelings for Noah were too big a problem to be faced tonight. Tomorrow would be soon enough.

'We still need to talk, Cate.' Noah's voice came from behind her and Cate's heart thumped, a strange feeling, similar to the one she'd felt before getting into the helicopter. She turned slowly and faced him.

His face was all harsh planes and angles. She couldn't do this now. 'I did consider it, Noah, but I'm tired—'

He stepped up beside her and cut off her words. 'I know you are. We're both tired, but I would appreciate it if you would step into my office for a moment.'

His eyes held hers and she tried to look away but couldn't. She remembered the relief she'd felt when he'd appeared on the riverbank and even the thought of him while she'd been in the boat. She walked past him into the office.

The sound of the door as he shut it behind her made her heart thump again.

Noah walked to the window, stared out for a moment and then turned to face her. His eyes bored into hers. 'Are you considering going back to Dwyer?'

Cate had had enough. 'The man's mother died this morning. I don't think this is a good time to discuss my relationship with him.' What was Noah's problem now? When it all boiled down, she'd kissed Noah twice and he thought he owned her. She stamped down the thought of what kisses they'd been... Her chin came up. 'What makes you think it's any of your business, anyway?'

'I'm sorry about Mrs Dwyer. I know she was your friend.' He stepped towards her until there was only a hand's breadth between them. Despite her body screaming for escape, she refused to step back.

He ran his hand through his hair and his eyes softened. 'But I decided you are my business when I thought I'd lost you in the river today.' He stepped closer until her vision was blocked by his body and she felt the barest touch of his chest against her breasts. A shudder ran through her body and his voice was barely above a whisper. 'And it became my business after I held you and kissed you today.'

Cate tipped her head back to look at him and typically, when she was too close to Noah, her mind worked sluggishly. It was hard to think when all she wanted to do was lose herself in his arms and recapture the taste of him. Then her mind cleared.

Lose herself! Her half-closed eyes snapped open. This was getting out of her control. She needed to remind herself there was little hope of a future in this relationship. He was going back to Sydney soon. She tried for flippancy. 'I thought the kissing was mutual. I'd hate you to take all the credit.'

His teeth snapped together. 'If that's the case, why were you kissing Dwyer?'

So that's what all this was about. Men! Her own temper surfaced as the implications set in. Cate stepped back and looked meaningfully towards the window that faced the car park. 'Doing a spot of peeping Tommery, Noah? Is that what all this is about? Dog in a manger?'

His eyes glittered and she stepped back a fraction. 'I think we have more than that between us.' He bit the words out and spun away from her. Cate drew a deep breath at the sudden space around her. She saw him roll his shoulders to ease the tension in his neck and she remembered he'd been in the helicopter, too. She imagined it might almost have been harder to watch than experience—especially if he was beginning to care for her. How did she feel about that? She realised she'd never really thought about how he might be affected by all this.

He turned back to face her and he smiled ruefully at her. Slowly, but with purpose, he leant down and very softly brushed her lips with his.

'I'm sorry. It's been a big day for both of us. And I'm rushing you.'

He kissed her again.

Not fair, Cate thought as another shudder ran through her body. She tried to stay rigid and unmoved beneath his insidious onslaught. If he used force she could push him away, slap his face and get out of there. But this was a dare—a challenge to stay unmoved as with the barest whisper his lips paid homage to her mouth and her brow and jaw, and it was the most difficult thing in the world for Cate to fight against.

And Noah knew it.

She could feel his breath against her face and the beginnings of his abrasive bristles rasped across her cheek. His thick, curling lashes rested on his cheeks—lashes that any woman would have given her eye teeth for. They didn't match his businesslike veneer and gave him a vulnerability that was at odds with what she knew of him. Vulnerability that she found achingly attractive, and it didn't help to keep her immune from his power. She needed more time.

She could feel herself softening against him and the moment had come to either bail out or admit to him that he could move her more than she wanted him to.

She stepped back.

He opened his eyes and she almost lost herself in their sleepy passion. He stroked her cheek. 'I never took you to be a coward, Cate.' The warmth in his eyes caressed her. 'Admit we have something special going on here.'

Cate panicked. 'Why? So you can slum it with the country bumpkin?' She was backed into a corner and she knew it. But she wasn't going to admit to anything when she wasn't even sure how she felt. She'd done that with Brett. She wouldn't let herself be seduced into a relationship that should never be.

Noah gripped her arms as if he wanted to shake her. 'Dammit, Cate, can't you see this is no game? When this is all over we need to talk about the rest of our lives.' He took a shaky breath. 'I want you to come back to Sydney with me. We should be together.'

That completely floored her. After all she'd gone through with Brett, here she was, receiving another offer to be a Sydney doctor's wife. Assuming Noah *was* talking marriage. How did she get herself into these situations? He'd expect her to leave everything she loved and held dear, desert her friends and colleagues at her hospital and play happy housewife to Noah in Sydney. After knowing him for less than a week! 'I can't' was all she could manage, but a tiny part inside her was tired of fighting the strength of her feelings for Noah and urged her to listen.

'That's not the answer I wanted,' he said as his arms dropped to his sides. Weak tears hovered behind Cate's eyes. Confusion and indecision wasn't like her and she hated the feeling. Disgusted with herself, Cate needed to get away. She turned on her heel, flung open the door and almost ran down the corridor.

She'd never run from anyone in her life and she hated the thought that Noah had seen her run from him.

Monday 12 March

After a restless night's sleep, Cate woke to bright sunlight. Even Point Lookout had had barely three millilitres of rain. The highway was still cut off and would be for days, but the water was going down in the town centre. Emergency vehicles could even drive through some of the streets.

The schools were still closed and, as expected, Amber was unable to come in. Cate worked the morning shift and tried to vary her routine to avoid seeing Noah. She wanted to sort out her feelings, and she reminded herself how short the time was that they'd known each other. She didn't need to rush. She didn't go down to breakfast and spent more time on the wards than in her office.

Now that the rain had ceased and the upriver levels were falling, the SES had the chance to offer to ferry hospital staff across the river. This allowed those who had worked to have a break and new volunteers to take extra shifts. The rooms in the nurses' home were vacated as staff moved more freely between home and work.

Wryly, Cate slipped a room key into an envelope and wrote Noah's name on it. At least he might get a better night's sleep in a proper bed.

All in all, the hospital appeared less of an outpost in the middle of a huge inland sea. The water covered the land in every direction and houses popped above the mirror-like surface like islands. Incredibly, morale was good.

Except in Cate's office. She wanted to go home, where she couldn't be rushed into something she wasn't sure of. She'd come perilously close to falling in love with Noah Masters, a city-bred, budget-conscious despot who agreed with the downgrading of her hospital—and expected to dominate her personally. She couldn't do it. So why did she still want to give him another chance?

The phone rang and Cate snatched it up with relief. It was Stella Moore. 'Big problems, Cate.' Cate switched modes as Stella went on. 'I've got young Barry Kelso, Jim Kelso's ten-year-old boy, with severe abdominal pain and a white cell count of twenty-six thousand. The resident thinks he's about to rupture his appendix. He needs to go to Theatre pronto and they don't think an airlift would get him to another hospital quick enough.'

Cate frowned. 'But we've already got one theatre going and I don't have more theatre staff on duty—or a surgeon, for that matter. So we're better to fly him out.'

Stella wasn't having it. 'You can be the scrub nurse, and what about Masters? You told me he trained as a surgeon in Sydney. It's not a big operation but if that appendix blows we're going to have one sick kid. He needs attention now.'

Cate thought quickly and weighed up the chances of arranging a second theatre team. If Stella thought time was that critical then it was. 'Get the resident to ring Dr Masters and I'll see if I can find a scout nurse at least. Ring me back with his answer.' She ran her finger down the list of staff on duty and located one of the nurses who usually worked in the theatres doing a shift in the medical ward. She called Stella back and confirmed that surgery would take place.

Cate looked at her watch. 'Prep Barry and send him around to Theatre. I've sent a nurse inside to start a set-up in Theatre two and hopefully Dr Masters will have organised an anaesthetist.' Cate grabbed her pager and pulled the office door shut behind her. She was too tired for this. She hadn't worked in Theatres for twelve months and she wasn't looking forward to working with Noah.

But she needn't have worried. Noah only spoke

to her when absolutely necessary. He looked pale and tense and she felt a prick of concern and that niggly feeling again.

The resident was an able assistant, which made Cate's job easier. But she hated the loss of rapport that she'd been used to with Noah.

As she handed the special appendix forceps to Noah they could all see how careful he would have to be. The bloated offender hovered on the brink of exploding as it was tied off and severed from its anchor. A chain reaction of sighs reverberated around the room when the inflamed tube of tissue lay harmlessly in the kidney dish.

Noah, internally at least, allowed himself to relax. It had been even harder than he'd imagined to force himself to operate. When he'd entered the room fully scrubbed, they'd all been waiting for him, and the fact that it had been two years since he'd picked up a scalpel had crashed in on him.

The ghost of Donna had seemed to hover in front of the table until the moment he'd seen Cate's eyes above her mask and then, strangely, his wife had disappeared. But not the nerves.

His surgical skills had returned with gradually increasing ease and he remembered he'd always enjoyed Theatre work until that last time—but he'd still damned Cate for placing him in this position.

In fact, damn Cate for forcing him into a lot of things he hadn't planned on, like falling in love with a woman who didn't love him. And damn himself for being so irrational!

Now that the surgical danger was past he just wanted to get out of there. He couldn't stand the bleakness he saw in Cate's eyes above her mask. He'd only glanced at her once during the operation and that had been his only fumble.

Closure was fast and neat, and before Cate knew it Noah was leaving the theatres. He didn't even look her way as he pushed open the door, and she was surprised how much that hurt.

There was a sudden lessening of tension in the room with his departure and the scout nurse cracked a joke, which the anaesthetist appreciated anyway. Cate just smiled tiredly.

Noah was an accomplished surgeon as well as an excellent diagnostician. And he didn't want to use either skill. She wished she knew why. Still, they were all grateful he'd been there today. Cate tidied the theatres on autopilot. There was so much she didn't know about Noah and some things she'd been wrong about. How far-fetched was the idea that they could make a life together?

When she left the theatres, she turned towards the gardens. She needed fresh air and a moment to gather herself. Apparently, so had Noah.

Cate hesitated, but then he looked up from the bench he was sitting on and stood up.

'Have a seat for a moment, Cate. Please.' The dappled sunlight cast shadows on his face and she thought he looked tired and, strangely, almost defeated.

She didn't say anything, just perched on the end of the bench, and he sat down beside her. She waited for him to speak and the leaves rustled with the light breeze to fill the silence. He didn't look at her when he asked the question so it took her by surprise.

'Tell me about your engagement to Dwyer.' It was the last thing she'd expected him to say.

Cate looked at the backs of her hands and her ringless fingers. There was no reason he shouldn't know. 'My engagement was a mistake. I entered into it for all the wrong reasons and thankfully Brett broke it off when I refused to go to Sydney with him.' She turned her head towards Noah. 'I thought what we had would be enough, along with a family, for me to be happy. But it wouldn't have been.'

She met Noah's eyes. 'Was your marriage what you expected?'

He sighed. 'My wife died two years ago. It was the worst day of my life.' Cate winced at the pain in her heart that statement caused. Of course he'd loved his wife.

Noah went on in a curious flat tone that showed he preferred not to think about these memories. 'The day started normally enough. We had another argument, another nail in the coffin of our two-year marriage. She wanted extensions to the house, and I felt like we'd just got rid of the last lot of builders living in the place.' He grimaced wryly. 'Stupid reasons to fight but our married life seemed to end up like that.'

He sighed. 'We didn't have enough in common and should never have drifted into that marriage. I regret we wasted so much of the time we should have enjoyed before she died.'

He rubbed the palms of his hands on his trousers. 'That day I left for work with arguments unresolved, and I remember feeling as guilty as hell, but I still left. That was the last time I saw her alive.' Cate lay her hand over his and he went on.

'When I got to work, I buried myself in the chaos.' He shook his head. 'Work shouldn't shield you from the responsibilities of your family. I had a responsibility to put my wife first.' Cate could see he'd almost forgotten she was there.

'Donna and our hassles were soon swallowed by the influx of emergencies. When the moment came it was like so many others that I didn't even have a premonition. There were two motor vehicle accident victims—emergency tracheostomy for a child, followed by the resuscitation of a woman in her twenties. We worked on the child first and by the time we started on the woman she was almost dead. That's when I found out it was Donna. She'd driven her car into another one and I have to believe her carelessness was because of the way I left her.'

'You can't know that.' Cate closed her eyes briefly at the pain in his voice and she couldn't help shifting closer to him to offer what comfort she could.

'Donna died and I was the one who lost her.'

Cate opened her mouth to speak but he must have sensed her intention because his eyes implored her to let him finish.

'It all happened so fast. Obviously, if there had been the resources and the time, I would have arranged for another doctor to take over her care, rather than be responsible myself. But there wasn't time. We rushed her to Theatre and we tried frantically to stop the bleeding, but it wasn't good enough.' He shook his head and his voice was flat. 'I wasn't good enough. I still don't know, if she'd been someone I hadn't been emotionally involved with, whether I would have been able to save her, or if it had always been hopeless.'

He looked around at the garden and then back at Cate. 'I've been living in a vacuum for the last two years. The guilt changed me. It wasn't my fault or that of any of the staff on that day. It was the fault of inadequate funds for staffing at major hospitals. But I couldn't allow myself to be placed in that situation again. Someone more influential than a director of casualty needed to address those issues. I decided I would see that it was done—for Donna and others like her.'

He shrugged. 'For the next eighteen months I shut myself off from social contact and concentrated on the fight to ensure that adequate staffing and funding would be directed towards hospitals with greater workloads.'

He shrugged again. 'In administration, I did make progress. When I was seconded to oversee the amalgamation of New South Wales regional hospitals, I felt I had a chance to ensure that funds were diverted to the areas that needed them most.'

He looked down at Cate and smiled at her. 'My crowning conceit was the short time I assumed I would need to sort out these tiny outposts of inefficiency.'

Cate gave a wry chuckle and he raised his brows ruefully.

'I knew it was only a temporary post, but if I managed to initiate the changes that my weak-kneed predecessors hadn't been able to achieve, with those credentials behind me I could make a difference where it really counted. Somewhere it affected a major city so that what had happened to Donna and others would never happen again.'

He smiled down at her. 'I thought I'd start with Riverbank. Thank God I did. I met this gorgeous, war-like creature who stood up for her hospital and showed me that Emergency facilities are needed everywhere—city and country.'

Cate closed her eyes as she felt a rush of understanding, and of relief. Then she ventured a comment. 'Do you still feel you can't practise medicine?'

'Tenacious as always.' Noah looked at her. 'I'm

not ruling it out.' He stood up and he stared down at her as if imprinting her face on his memory. 'That's all I wanted to say, Cate. I hope now you can see why I've done what I've done, said what I've said, and that you don't hate me too much.' And then he left her.

She stared at the spot where he'd disappeared through the doors. *Now* what did she think?

She felt like she was on an out-of-control train rushing down a hill and she wasn't sure if she wanted to strap herself in or jump off before it was too late. She needed time out.

She went to see Sylvia and played dolls for half an hour until Gladys came for a brief visit to her daughter.

Cate returned to her office and, of course, the phone was ringing. Lately, she'd almost felt like throwing the thing against the wall. It was definitely time to have a few days off.

It was Amber. After the pleasantries to which Cate lied and said she was fine, Amber dropped her bombshell. 'Brett has offered to babysit Cindy so that I can work Tuesday.'

Cate's eyes widened. 'Do you think he's in a fit state of mind to do that?'

Amber was serious. 'He says it will keep him busy and he wants to.'

'He's always been good with kids,' Cate agreed, and wondered what else was going on. But it was none of her business. Amber knew Brett's failings and he did have good points. Cate just didn't appreciate them and obviously Amber did. It would take some getting used to but the idea wasn't crazy.

Amber rang off and Cate replaced the receiver. She could go home at the end of this shift. Tonight. If she could find someone with a boat to take her. Amber would work tomorrow's shift.

Susie's Pete was more than happy to drop Cate off on his way home after she'd finished work. It all became too easy. She didn't see Noah, although she hesitated outside his office again. She heard his deep voice on the phone and continued past. She wasn't rushing into anything. It was better this way.

When she stepped off Pete's boat not far from the doorstep of her parents' house, it felt strange to be home, almost as if she didn't belong there any more.

Water stretched in every direction and the fences had disappeared beneath the surface. The late afternoon sun had turned the expanse of water to burnished copper and for such destruction it held incredible beauty.

Then her mother came down the verandah steps and enveloped her in a hug. 'Welcome to Forrest Island, darling,' she said with a laugh, and Cate didn't feel so strange.

Cate hugged her back and they moved onto the verandah. Her father rolled out in his wheelchair with Ben behind him and they crowded around Cate. She realised that Ben had grown and there was no doubt he was now a man. She'd have to stop bossing him around, that was for sure. Maybe it was time for him to stay and her to go.

'So, did you organise the hospital the way you wanted to?' Ben teased.

Cate bit her lip. 'Actually, they had a new CEO who did a pretty good job, but tell me all the news from here.'

They pulled her inside to sit around the kitchen table and the Primus stove was on the bench with a billy of tea bubbling away. The power was still off. They discussed the work involved to get the farm back on its feet once the water receded. The farm had lost all the winter hay bales, most of the fences were damaged and the tractor would have to be stripped and rebuilt, but it was all doable.

William shrugged. 'Nature decides when we need a clean-out and we'll salvage what we can and be sorted out in a few months. I'm pleased for your mother that the water didn't come into the house. And it's good to have you both home.'

Later she and Ben had a heart to heart. When she asked why he'd left he met her eyes ruefully. 'Because you always seemed to be able to do everything better than I could. And I couldn't stand it.'

Cate squeezed his shoulder. 'I'm ten years older than you are. You're a man now, Ben, and we're equal. We don't have to compete and I don't even want to. Me not being here for the flood worked well for both of us.'

She gazed out the window at the water stretching

into the distance. 'I had to be strong for Dad but I'm tired of being responsible. Who knows? If you stay I might have time for my own life.'

Ben looked at her with new understanding. 'I never thought of you as being tired, but I guess you have carried the farm with Mum for a long time.' He hugged her. 'I want to stay. I've missed the farm but I've learnt new skills that I can use here.'

So everything worked out in the end, Cate thought. Except she didn't know what she wanted any more. Perhaps she just needed her bed. Noah's flood had exhausted her. But it was the man and not the flood that filled her thoughts as she drifted into sleep.

Tuesday 13 March

The sun was rising when Cate woke and she stretched luxuriantly in her own comfortable bed. When she turned her head to look out of her window, the golden pink dawn sent shimmering rays of multicoloured light to reflect off the expanse of water. Great flocks of white and black ibises lined the edge of the water as they enjoyed their breakfast, and cattle jostled for position around the hay bales Ben had left.

Cate hadn't stirred all night and as she sat up she felt refreshed and ready to face the day. And Noah. He'd been right. She had been a coward. How long was the right length of time if you've met your soul-mate? One week, one month, one year? It didn't matter if you couldn't imagine them leaving. Noah had said he wanted to talk and she should have listened. It wasn't too late to tell him how she felt.

She got up and padded down the hallway before lifting the upstairs phone and dialling his direct number. She could feel the smile on her face, and she wondered if he was still angry with her. A bubble of anticipation simmered away inside as she waited for him to answer. She listened to the phone in his office ringing and then she was cut off.

Disappointed, but not surprised he wasn't there, she dialled the main hospital number and asked the switchboard operator to page him for her.

The receptionist's voice was bored, as if she'd passed this message on several times already. 'Mr Masters is unavailable. A Mr Brown has taken over in the interim but it's Tuesday and he's not in. Would you like to leave a message?'

Cate bit her lip. 'No. Thank you. Goodbye.'

Unavailable? What did that mean? He'd gone? Without a word?

But so did you, she reminded herself, and she sat carefully on the hallway stool and thought about the consequences and what control she had over the situation.

She phoned Amber at work. She needed to tell Noah that she was ready to talk about their future together. Amber would know where he was.

CHAPTER NINE

'CATE, I'm so glad you rang.' Amber sounded anything but glad and her voice shook. With a flutter of alarm, Cate remembered the last time Amber had been reluctant to pass on news.

Cate tightened her grip on the phone. It had to be something to do with Noah. 'I'm glad you're glad. Now, tell me what's made you sound odd before I start imagining things are even worse than they are.'

Amber's voice wavered. 'It's been terrible. We had a fire in the children's ward last night.' She paused as if to collect herself. 'It was a very close call. One of the patients' older brothers was playing with matches. When the curtains caught alight it took over faster than anyone could believe.'

Cold dread filled Cate's stomach as she imagined the horror of what could have happened, and icy fingers recalled Sylvia with oxygen beside her bed. 'Tell me none of the kids were injured?'

'Sylvia's been treated for smoke inhalation and if Noah hadn't been reading to her, she would have been in real danger of being burnt to death.' There was a catch in Amber's voice and she was still noticeably upset. 'He carried her through a wall of flame that should have killed them both. I know you don't like him, but he's a hero, Cate, and nobody will listen to anything bad about him from now on.'

Cate's face felt wooden. Was that really what people thought? That she didn't even *like* the man she loved? Was that what *Noah* thought? A cold panic settled in her stomach as she struggled to get the situation straight in her head. 'So is Sylvia all right?'

'Yes.' Amber's voice trailed off.

'And Noah? Is he all right?' Cate tasted the blood from her lip and realised how hard she'd bitten it as she waited. *Come on, Amber, stop stalling. I'm going insane here.*

'He will be. He has second-degree burns to his hands but they think there will be no lasting damage.'

Cate sagged against the wall. 'Thank God for that. And smoke inhalation?'

'No. His lungs are fine. It's—it's his eyes.'

Cate felt like screaming. 'What about his eyes, Amber? Where is he?'

'His eyes were damaged and they're not certain if his sight is going to be badly affected. They flew him out last night in one of the helicopters to St Vincent's in Sydney.'

Cate didn't say anything. Couldn't. Just leant against the wall and tried to imagine big, strong, in-control Noah blindfolded and with both hands bandaged.

'Are you there, Cate?' Amber's voice squeaked

down the phone, and Cate pushed the pictures from her head and tried to work out a plan of action.

'Yes. I'm here.' She rubbed her brow. 'Listen, Amber. Has Noah's family been notified?' She shook her head at her own lack of knowledge. 'I don't even know if he has family or even a house in Sydney. He must have one or the other. Find out for me. I'll try and get a lift to the hospital and I'll catch up with you then.'

Cate hung up and when she turned around her mother was standing there.

Leanore put her arm around Cate. 'What's happened, darling?'

'A fire at the hospital. Noah is hurt. He's been taken to Sydney and I need to go to him.'

'Noah, the domineering, human logarithm who works out?' She smiled gently at her daughter. 'You're in love with him, aren't you?'

Cate gave a small hiccup of laughter at Leanore's infallible memory and her disorientation settled. Was she in love with Noah? She looked at her mother. 'I guess I must be. I can't bear the thought of him disabled and defenceless. I have to be there for him.'

'Then I'll phone Susie's Pete again while you pack.'

The boat ride was uneventful, and even though the highway was still cut off and the planes were grounded, the trains were still running. Cate was able to secure a seat on the train to Sydney for later that morning.

Amber had found Noah's address but no evidence of next of kin. She'd taken one look at Cate's face and put her hand over her mouth. 'You're in love with him.'

'Yes. And he asked me to go back to Sydney with him.' Cate swallowed the lump in her throat.

Amber was wide-eyed. 'And you said you'd go?'

Cate turned away. 'I'm still here, aren't I? But I was a fool. I'd follow that man anywhere.' She looked at Amber. 'I have to go. I love him and he needs me.'

When Cate stepped down from the train at Central Station in Sydney it was late in the afternoon, coming up to peak-hour traffic and raining. She carried her case easily, a tall, confident woman in jeans and oilskin, her black Squatter Akubra hat resting comfortably on her head.

Some Japanese tourists smiled and waved and took a photo and Cate supposed she had farmer written all over her. She waved back and anxiously strode over to a waiting taxi.

'St Vincent's Hospital, please,' she told the cabby, and sat back to stare out of the window. She tried to glimpse the sky above the buildings that stretched up out of sight. She'd been to Sydney several times as a child to watch her father compete at the Royal Easter Show, but the tall buildings and the multiculturalism, compared to Riverbank, never failed to amaze her.

When the taxi pulled up at the hospital, she paid the driver and alighted at the huge entrance. She supposed there must be bigger hospitals but, compared to Riverbank, it was a monster.

She hurriedly followed the signs to Reception to ask to speak to Noah's doctor. Noah was under the care of an eminent ophthalmologist and Cate was allowed to speak to the great man's registrar.

Half an hour later she was standing outside Noah's room and the determination that had seen her through the long journey suddenly dried up and disappeared.

What if he didn't want to see her? What if there was some other woman in the wings? She should have asked the doctor that, too. Noah's wife had been dead for two years—it was possible there was someone else. Cate lifted her hat and ran her fingers through her hair. Well, standing out here wasn't doing anyone any good. She opened the door, picked up her case and walked in softly.

The curtains over the window were pulled and no one had been in to turn the light on yet. Her first glance had gone to the bed but it was empty. Then she saw that he was sitting in the armchair beside the window. He'd turned his head towards the door when she'd entered. His eyes and both hands were heavily bandaged. Cate's throat closed and her voice choked on the greeting she'd been about to offer.

She could have lost him before she'd even appreciated what she'd found. She hoped he still wanted her.

'I'm not really in the mood for an examination right now.' Noah's voice was resigned and more hoarse than usual. She supposed it was from the smoke. The thought of him being hurt was too much and she crossed the room and knelt beside the chair.

She swallowed and tried to moisten her dry mouth. 'Hello, Noah.'

'Cate?' He smelt the rain on her oilskin and the herbal scent that she liked. She'd come. Noah averted his face. He'd been wishing for and dreading the possibility of her arrival. She was the woman he wanted to spend the rest of his life with—but not if he was blind. The thought of vital Cate tied to him as an invalid horrified him.

He hated her to see him like this but it was too late now. Her presence reminded him that if he lost his sight he would lose more than that. 'What are you doing here?' His voice was harsh with the see-sawing scenarios in his mind.

Cate wanted to grab his hand and hold it to her cheek, but his body language repelled any advances. She rested her hand on her own thigh instead as she knelt in front of him. 'I came when I heard. I thought you'd like to know that Sylvia is fine and going home tomorrow. And everyone is calling you a hero.'

He cursed his inability to walk around the room

so she couldn't read his face, though he supposed most of his features were bandaged. He grimaced at the memory of the last time he'd tried to pace. That would be all he needed to complete his ignominy—to trip over a stool and fall flat on his face in front of her. The worst thing she could give him would be pity.

Damn this contrary woman! She wouldn't come when he wanted or stay away when she should. 'You could have phoned to tell me all that. There's nothing wrong with my ears.' His voice was cold.

'So you *can* hold a phone, can you?' There was emotion in her voice but he couldn't tell if it was anger or distress. She seemed to be ignoring his bad humour, and perversely that made him more angry.

'Low blow, Cate. No, I can't hold anything.' Not even you, he thought bitterly. When she didn't retaliate he shrugged, settled back in the chair and turned his face towards her. 'So what really brought Country Cate to the big, bad city?'

He heard her shift beside him and thought it was one of the few times he'd managed to discomfit her. Then her beautiful voice came from beside him and he could imagine the way her lips moved and the expressions on her face, and suddenly the picture in his memory made him want to bury his face in her neck and hide. He loved her and that was why he hadn't wanted her to come.

'I came because I needed to know that you're all right.' Her voice was quiet. 'I see that you will live, despite the bandages, but your manners could do with improving.'

Noah couldn't stand much more of this. He had to drive her away before he weakened and begged her to stay. 'Well, I'm glad *one* of us can see. My apologies for not standing up when you came in, but I tend to fall over.' He gave a short, sharp laugh and he felt Cate flinch beside him.

It was better to hurt her now than later. 'Listen, Cate. Go home. I don't want you or need you here. This is my town. I want you to go back where you belong.' There, he'd said it. Now he wished she'd leave him to be miserable in private.

There was a long silence before she said, almost in a whisper, 'I don't believe you, Noah.' Her voice was expressionless and she stood up and walked around the room.

Her footsteps stopped in front of him. 'How about I tell you what I think you should do and you listen?'

Noah snorted. Already she thought she could decide what was best for him. The next thing she'd be wanting to mother him. He'd throw himself out the window first. His voice was soft but brooked no argument. 'Be careful, Cate. Even blind and without the use of my hands, nobody tells me what to do, not even you.'

Unfortunately she didn't sound impressed. 'Well, I don't think you have much choice here, Noah. I've spoken to your doctor. If you have a carer, me, you can be discharged in a couple of days. Of course, that depends if the result is good when the eyepads come off tomorrow. Or you can stay here. Alone. Bored silly. Morose as hell until your hands heal in a week or more.'

Her voice softened. 'Why don't you let me stay so that I can take you home when you're ready? We can spar for the next couple of weeks and I'm sure the time would go more quickly.' She crouched down beside him and laid her hand on his leg. The warmth from her fingers soaked into him and he almost lifted his own hand to lay it over the top of hers until he remembered the bandages. What if his sight was permanently damaged? A picture of her leading him around his own house burst into his brain, like a Technicolor horror movie.

'No way!' The passion in his voice shocked both of them, and Cate sat back unsteadily. He tacked on a belated 'No, thank you' but it didn't change his vehemence.

Cate had known Noah could prove difficult to convince but this was daunting. He was dependent and he'd hate that. She'd even be pleased if he started to boss her around again—as long as he didn't tell her to go. She now knew that Noah was loving, caring, passionate, that he didn't want to dominate her, as she had feared. Sure, he was strong-willed and determined to be master of his own life, but that was just another reason why she loved him. It felt good just saying that to herself. She loved him. It gave her strength.

She smiled to herself. Perhaps this wasn't a good time to tell Noah, though. She squared her shoulders. He should have remembered who he was up against.

She stood and looked around to see where she'd put her case. 'Well, that was a definite answer. I guess I'll just have to keep coming back until you agree.'

Exasperated, Noah clenched his hands, and then swore at the pain he'd caused when he'd squeezed his fingers together. 'For heaven's sake, Cate. Can't you see I don't want you here? I don't want you seeing me like this and I don't want to have you caring for me when I'm weaker than a child.'

Cate wished she could share his pain, but she stopped herself from softening. She was just as determined as he could be, and she had to be strong for him.

'It's *because* of a child you *are* here. Sylvia owes her life to you.'

He snorted. 'So that's why you're here? Because of Sylvia?'

Cate gently poked his leg. 'No. That's not why I'm here, you big oaf, but we'll talk about that later.' Then she stroked his thigh. 'And why the hell can't I look after you? You need daily dressings—I'm a nurse. I'm experienced and quite strong. I can't see a line-up of people waiting for the job, Noah, so accept my help graciously and get us both out of here. Sooner rather than later.'

There was silence in the room. He didn't answer and she stared at the rain running down the window.

Finally, he leaned his head closer to where he could hear her voice and his weariness was clear. 'You don't get it. Do you? I don't care where I am and I want to be alone.'

Cate bit her lip but refused to be daunted. 'Alone isn't an option, Noah. I'm staying in Sydney for the next few days at least.'

He rose shakily to his feet but there was no waver in the bandaged fist that pointed to the door. 'Out. Please.'

Cate swallowed the lump in her throat as she watched him feel his way to the bed. He looked so helpless and she could only guess how much he must hate that. Her voice was thick with tears and she hoped he didn't notice. Maybe he hadn't because he continued to awkwardly climb onto the bed.

'I'm sorry if I upset you by coming, Noah,' she said. 'But I'm not going home until after you see the doctor tomorrow and we know the prognosis for your sight.' She picked up her hat and her case. 'I'll go and find the YWCA for the night but I'll be back tomorrow. And the next day if you need me. And the next. And we'll face what the doctor says together. Then, if you still want to send me away, I'll go. But I'm not leaving Sydney before I'm ready.'

He didn't answer and he heard the door shut behind her. To torture himself, he pictured her as she'd looked that night they'd played pool. Long legs and blonde hair and her smile. And the way she'd moved around the pool table and the way she'd made him feel. And he couldn't even punch anything because his hands still felt like someone was running a blowtorch over them.

He heard the door open and the click of the light switch. For a moment he thought Cate had come back and, despite himself, he felt his heart skip with excitement. Then the nurse swished in. He recognised her sound and then her voice as he felt an aching disappointment.

'It's Karen, the nurse. How's the pain, Mr Masters?' She was young, he guessed, but she was competent. And she'd put up with his growling. 'I'm just going to lift your hands to see if there's any seepage through the bandage.' She did what she'd said and he let her. She mumbled something he didn't hear.

She rested his hands carefully back on his chest. 'Here's two pain tablets the doctor wants you to have every four hours—but remember, if the pain breaks through, you can have something stronger.' She helped him sit up and popped the tablets into his mouth and then he felt the straw against his mouth. He submitted because last time he'd said he'd do it himself he'd lost the tablets in the bed and had managed to wet his bandaged hands. At least Cate hadn't seen that.

'Thank you,' Noah said. He had a sudden vision of Cate in the streets of unfamiliar Sydney and a great twist of fear speared his gut. What had he been thinking? 'Is it dark outside?'

'Yes, it is. It's still raining, too,' Karen said.

Maybe they could stop her. 'My friend. The one who was here. Has she gone yet?'

'The lady with the black hat…' The nurse stopped and Noah smiled grimly to himself. Of course, he hadn't seen the hat but that was Cate all right. 'I'm sorry,' she said.

'It's okay. She always wears it so I knew who you were talking about. She said she was going to the YWCA. I'd like her to come back if you can catch her, please.'

There was doubt in the nurse's voice. 'She went down in the lift before I came in. And there's a taxi rank outside the hospital. I'll ring Reception but I don't think they'll catch her, Mr Masters.' She hurried out.

Noah sat tense and waiting and more worried about missing Cate than what he was going to say if she came back.

But it was the nurse who came back. 'I'm sorry, Mr Masters. The receptionist did see her get into a taxi. She's a striking woman and hard to miss.'

'Thank you.' He heard the door close after the nurse and Noah slumped back against the pillows.

Yes, Cate was a striking woman. And fair game for any creep on the streets. He'd been lying here, feeling sorry for himself, and now Cate was out in the night life of Sydney, alone and country green.

If anything happened to her, it would be a hundred times worse than the position he was in at the moment.

And it would be his fault. How could he have been so stupid not to have foreseen this when she'd said she was going? Pride. Stupid pride.

He disgusted himself. It was just like his reaction after Donna died. He was going to save the world. Sydney hospitals were going to benefit and the smaller, less important ones would be downgraded to pay for it. As long as major centres took acute cases, all needs would be met. But Cate had shown him that the needs and the heart of every hospital were equal.

Emergencies would come and go in every town, regardless of size, and there would never be enough funding to go around. But if his sight returned and he could work, he would protect Riverbank and places like it from people like himself who didn't understand. Maybe not him and Cate together, but he would do it because now he understood.

Tonight all he could do was ask them to ring the Y in an hour and check if Cate had booked in. He couldn't lie here and wonder if she was all right. He'd go insane.

*   *   *

Cate didn't even give the night life of Sydney a second thought. She wasn't stupid. She stepped from the taxi and crossed the footpath to enter the sliding doors of the large YWCA in the centre of Sydney. She'd stayed here with her mother while her dad had slept at the showground all those years ago. It looked pretty similar, though maybe a little more drab, but it was somewhere she felt at ease. Most of the guests were from the country.

She registered at the desk and ordered a take-away meal from the restaurant to eat in her room.

She had heard the way Noah had said her name when she'd first gone into his hospital room. There was no doubting he'd been pleased before he'd thought about it. Then his stupid pride had stood in the way. But who was she to talk? When she thought of the opportunities she'd wasted at the hospital she was no better.

She had to believe she could beat his reluctance to have her around.

CHAPTER TEN

Wednesday 14 March

THE next morning, Noah didn't hear Cate open the door because he was swearing at a piece of toast that kept slipping out of his bandaged hands.

'That's no way to talk to your breakfast. Let me cut it for you.' Her voice floated across the room and the tension in his neck disappeared. He hadn't driven her away. He couldn't feel sorry. He needed her today when the doctor came.

He dropped the toast again and the crumbs went down his shirt. But he didn't care. Thank God she was safe.

Of course she was safe. She was probably capable of throwing a hog tie on any mugger that had the audacity to accost her. His Cate.

'I'm sure, if you'd waited, someone would have come in to help you.' She had her nursing supervisor voice on now and it brought back good memories of the last week. Anything to take his mind off the doctor's visit this morning.

'Well, don't just stand there—butter the thing, please! I hate dry toast.' He gave a little chuckle and Cate felt a wave of relief wash over her. She buttered and cut the toast and brushed his lip with a piece. 'Your toast, sir.'

Noah opened his mouth and she popped it in. While he chewed, he tried to picture what she was wearing. But it really didn't matter. She'd look wonderful no matter what. He heard her pour the tea and then smelt the tealeaves. Everything took time to happen when he couldn't do it himself. Blindness meant compulsory listening and he could even hear Cate breathe.

She was very good at feeding him. 'Thank you, slave,' he teased. 'I think you should be feeding me grapes.'

'You're welcome, Noah.' She squeezed his wrist above the bandages. 'Of course I couldn't stay away when I knew I could have you in my power for a change.'

He rested back against the pillows. 'Is that so?' Enjoy it, then, because it's not going to last long, no matter what happens today.'

'We'll see,' she said. She straightened his pillow and a drift of her scent stayed behind on the pillowcase.

Then Noah heard the doctor's voice outside the room and he felt his skin go cold. All amusement disappeared. The time had come to find out just how visually impaired he was going to be. Cate took the breakfast tray away and rested her hand briefly on his leg. He was glad of the warmth and her support now, and he tried not to think about having to send her away if the prognosis was poor.

The door opened and the doctor came in. Cate took her hand from Noah's leg and stepped back from the bed, out of the way.

The doctor nodded to her on his way to his patient. 'Morning, Mr Masters. Morning, young lady.'

Cate could see that Noah wasn't up to pleasantries. His comment showed everyone else. 'Morning. Get it over with, please,' he growled, but the doctor seemed to understand.

'Impatient?' The specialist unwrapped the bandage from around Noah's head. 'Well, I can't say I blame you.' He looked at the sunlight streaming in the window and motioned to the nurse to pull the blinds. The room darkened considerably. 'As I said yesterday, the tests came back as positive news so I'm expecting a lot more vision than we originally hoped for.'

Cate saw Noah tighten his bandaged fists against his chest and she knew it must be hurting his damaged fingers. She could understand why he did it. Anything to distract himself. They all held their breath as the pads were lifted away from Noah's eyes. Noah kept them closed and Cate thought the suspense was going to make her sick.

She noted the redness from a heat sear across the upper half of Noah's face and the skin was peeling around his eyes. To Cate, it looked like the facial burns were mostly first degree, but his beautiful eyelashes and straight black brows were nearly all gone. She mentally shrugged. They'd grow back.

The jolliness was gone from the specialist's voice. 'I'll dab some saline over your eyelids to unstick them now.' He wiped both Noah's eyes carefully with special wet pads. 'All right, Mr Masters. Open your eyes.'

Tentatively, with jerky little movements, Noah stretched open his eyelids. It was too bright initially after the total dark under the bandages, and everything was wavy. He opened and shut his eyes gingerly a few times and slowly figures came into focus in the dark room. He saw the doctor for the first time, nothing like Noah had imagined from his hearty Swedish voice, and then he saw the nurse.

He couldn't see Cate. He turned his head and there she was against the wall, as beautiful as ever. Thank God. He sagged back in the pillows and closed his eyes. He could see.

'Well?' The doctor was leaning closer and with machiavellian nastiness he shone a small torch that made Noah flinch away. 'So they work!' He wrote on a notepad. 'How's the focus?'

Noah swore he would improve his own bedside manner if he ever worked as a doctor again. 'It's slow but it works.'

The doctor stepped back with a satisfied smile. 'Wear dark glasses for two weeks, and instil drops four times a day—the sister will give you the regime and a script to take home when you go.' He glanced at Noah's bandaged hands. 'These aren't my department. The eyes can go home tomorrow and come back to see me in four days for final tests. Good morning, to everyone.' And he departed. The nurse followed soon after and Noah and Cate were left alone.

Noah sighed and closed his eyes. He'd been incredibly lucky. He felt the bed shift as she hitched her hip on the edge. He remembered that hip. The back of his bandaged hand went down of its own accord and checked she was there.

She laughed and he loved the sound. 'Not only are you demanding but you're groping this morning. Have you decided it's not a bad thing I'm here now that your sight is restored?'

'I've decided that if my sight is as good as they expect, it might not be so bad to have you around and be my personal nurse.' He elbowed her gently. 'But I'm still the boss.'

'Really, Dr Masters?' She tapped his cheek with her finger. 'Open.' She put another piece of toast into his mouth.

Noah chewed and couldn't believe how light-hearted he felt. He felt as high as a kite. The next couple of days would be a pain but he could plan for after that.

He wasn't going to be blind and he could dare to dream of Cate again. The strain had been enormous and suddenly he was overwhelmingly tired. His eyelids grew heavy. It would all take time, he thought as he drifted off to sleep.

When Noah woke it was quite dark in the room with the blinds pulled, and his stomach told him it was well after lunch. Cate must have gone but he didn't doubt that she'd be back. By the time he'd struggled with his jocks in the adjoining bathroom, cleaned his teeth with the toothbrush between his wrists and stared at his two-day growth and hairless eyes, he was feeling depressed.

How on earth had he decided it was a good thing for Cate to see him like this?

Where was Cate? Noah walked through to his room and there she was, asleep like a gorgeous lioness in the chair by the window. There had been a time he'd thought he would never see anyone's face again, and it was Cate's he would have missed the most.

So should he send her away until he was normal again or should he live life to the full from the first possible moment?

Noah sat on the edge of the bed and stared at her. He brushed the blonde hair back off her forehead with his wrist and it felt like silk on his skin. He'd wanted to do that since he'd met her. She stirred and stretched, like the jungle cat she was, as she sleepily opened her eyes. 'Hello, beautiful,' he said. He hoped she wasn't repulsed by the face he'd just seen in the mirror.

'Hello, Noah.' And she smiled up at him. He felt

the weight lift from his shoulders. Cate stood up and came across to hug him. She couldn't believe how much she loved this man and she thanked God silently that Noah had survived the fire. She shivered and he looked down at her in concern.

'You OK?' He dropped a kiss on her forehead and she snuggled in tightly against him for a moment to gather herself. He smoothed her hair again. 'I'll be fine. I was so frightened when I heard you were hurt.'

He touched her lips with his bandaged hand to silence her when she went to speak again. He needed to do this now before something else went wrong. 'Shh. I need to say something.'

He leant across and kissed her gently on the lips. She stared up at him solemnly and it was all he could do not to kiss her again. But he knew he wouldn't stop if he started.

He drew a deep breath. It was time to be brave. 'Thank you for being here today. I need to tell you. I love you, Cate. I'll always love you. When I'm well again, will you marry me?'

Cate looked at Noah, her man, her soul-mate, and the love that shone from his eyes lifted any shadows of doubt from her mind. 'I'd follow you anywhere,' she said. 'I must have known instinctively that the respect and love I saw in my own home were missing from my relationship with Brett, but it's not like that with you. I love you, Noah. And I can't wait to be your wife.' She kissed him this time. 'And we'll have a wonderful life.'

They sealed their plans in a deeper kiss and Cate found the home that was hers whenever she was with Noah.

Later, when the room had righted and she lay comfortably against his shoulder high up on the hospital bed, she had a question. 'Where will we live? Do you have a house in Sydney?'

He kissed her again. 'I do but we'll sell it. I didn't choose the house. We could go back to Riverbank. It seems a great place to bring children up.' He watched her eyes light up and he knew he'd been blessed to find her. 'But I'm not a farmer, Cate,' he warned.

She laughed with delight. 'A house in town will be fine. I love you, Noah.'

CHAPTER ELEVEN

THREE months later the wedding was the social event of the year in Riverbank. The bride arrived in a horse-drawn carriage, accompanied by Amber and two flower-girls, Cindy and Sylvia.

When Cate entered the church beside her father's wheelchair, Noah didn't see the full church or the glorious flowers or even hear the music. His whole being was focused on this woman who matched him in every way. She looked like a queen—his queen—as she swayed regally towards him in a plain white sheath and a tiny flower-encrusted veil. He could see her beautiful lips curve beneath the edge of the veil and his fingers flexed in anticipation for when he would hold her hand in his and never let her go.

When their vows were complete, the church bells pealed over the valley. In shops and streets and houses, people smiled at the sound because most of the townsfolk knew who was being married today.

When Noah left the church with his new bride on his arm he understood that he was part of a larger family than he had bargained for. The love and welcome from Cate's mother and father and brother warmed a place in his heart that had been cold for too long. Noah smiled and nodded at the people he knew, like old Mrs Gorse. Mr and Mrs Ellis were there and even Paul the SES boat driver. Noah could watch and almost smile as Cate kissed Brett and his wife, Amber. Everywhere people knew his Cate and welcomed him.

At the reception, the ladies from the church had catered for a picnic for two hundred people. Tables were laid under the shade sails in front of Noah's and Cate's big house on the river and the country band played into the night.

Later, down on the jetty, in a patch of silver moonlight, Noah and Cate were oblivious to the music that drifted from the house. Held in Noah's strong arms, Cate had found her dream, and the reality of Noah's love was more beautiful than she could have hoped for. Beneath their feet, the river flowed gently past into the night and would do so every night to come.

'Welcome to your new home, Cate.' Noah's breath drifted across her cheek and she smiled.

'I noticed that our house has two stories—is that in case of floods, Dr Masters?'

'No. That's to hold all our children.' And his lips lowered to hers with the promise of a wonderful love that they would share for the rest of their lives.

Modern Romance™
...seduction and
passion guaranteed

Tender Romance™
...love affairs that
last a lifetime

Sensual Romance™
...sassy, sexy and
seductive

Blaze.
...sultry days and
steamy nights

Medical Romance™
...medical drama on
the pulse

Historical Romance™
...rich, vivid and
passionate

27 new titles every month.

*With all kinds of Romance for
every kind of mood...*

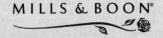

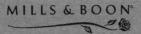

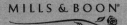